DAMNED RIGHT

DAMNED RIGHT

BAYARD JOHNSON

**BLACK ICE
BOOKS**

BOULDER • NORMAL

Published by FC2 with support given by the English
Department Unit for Contemporary Literature of Illinois
State University, the Illinois Arts Council, and the
National Endowment for the Arts

Address all inquiries to: FC2, Unit for Contemporary
Literature, Campus Box 4241, Illinois State Unversity,
Normal, IL 61790-4241

Damned Right
Bayard Johnson

ISBN: Paper. 0-932511-84-8, $7.95

Produced and printed in the United States of America

NATIONAL
ENDOWMENT
FOR THE
ARTS

This program is
partially supported by
a grant from the
Illinois Arts Council.

YEARS

For Atticus

Swift as many rivers streaming to the ocean,
Rush the heroes to your fiery gullets:
Mothlike, to meet the flame of their destruction,
Headlong these plunge into you, and perish.

> —from *The Song of God:*
> *BHAGAVAD-GITA*
> translated by
> Swami Prabhavananda
> and Christopher Isherwood

Now that Atticus is in prison there's nothing keeping me here. I always aimed to head for the bigtime anyway.

On the road through the mountains I keep it down to a reasonable speed. Somewhere around a hundred. 110 on the long straights. The two-lane backroads aren't where you hit 200 and beyond. They're not made for it. It's irresponsible.

The freeways are built for it. Their grace and curve and sweeping bankers. Their five-lane width. In Los Angeles I hear they have fourteen-laners, seven on each side. Maybe by now there are some sixteen-laners. They stay on top of it down there. It's the mecca of freeways. The center of the world. It's blasphemy to drive less than a hundred and sixty on roads like that. Sacrilege. That's why they're called freeways. It's on stretches like that you can be free in America. At 200 and beyond.

After the mountains comes the orchard country. It was desert before they bled the rivers dry. A cop sees me blur past at something over a hundred. I see his lights back there. I don't feel like stopping. If you don't feel like stopping you shouldn't stop. Some nerd in a uniform following you with flashing lights like a rolling Christmas ornament doesn't make it right. It's wrong to do things you don't want to do. Simple, right? A fascist with a pistol doesn't have any bearing on the morality of it. After all it's a free country.

I crank it up to around 160 and I don't see his lights any

9

more. The road isn't built for it though. I have that floating feeling. On the turns I have to slow it way down. The acceleration coming out of the curves makes it all worthwhile. You have to plan way ahead on a two-laner when you're passing cars and trucks that are going over a hundred miles an hour slower than you are. That's a major advantage of freeways, how all the lanes go the same way. It's much safer. Some junior jerk in the local gestapo is making me push the borders of safety. That's the trouble with having to be right. Sometimes you get stretched toward compromise. Compromise! I'm 26 years old but that won't last. I used to be 25 and someday I'll be dead. How can anyone compromise? By now the uniform is only a figment of my imagination so I ease back to 140. That's manageable. I can feel good about that.

I pass three more cops the same way. The last two are parked waiting for me but I burn them off. The highway leads north to the border and they might figure I'm headed there. Maybe they'll have a roadblock waiting.

When Orestes killed his mother he was tormented clear across the known world by a plague of flies. That's what they claim. Now they're swarming after me. Lying in wait up ahead. What's my terrible crime? I just want to see my sister on my way to the center of the known world. Since when was that a crime? You could feel desperate if you thought about it. Screw that. I refuse to feel like a criminal just because I'm treated like one. I'm no rebel. I'm just like you. I want what I want, that's all. I guess I just like to drive fast. I'm an American. I happen to live for speed. How can anyone compromise? I'm turning off before the border anyway.

Before the last American town I turn right off the main highway onto a state route. I turn right off the state route onto a paved county road. I turn right onto a gravel county road. The gravel is mixed with snow and the plows have piled dirty drifts on both sides. I flip a switch to raise the suspension. It's hydraulic. Atticus and I ripped off the idea from an old Citroen wagon. Why hadn't we ripped off the idea of a heater while we were at it? I won't need one when I get to L.A. though. Who needs the clutter?

A new car is stuck in the snow on a curve. She'd skidded off into the drifts. I stop and offer her a lift. She opens the passenger door.

"You'll have to sit on the floor," I say.

"Where's the other seats?"

"There's just the one." I'm sitting in it. "Sorry," I say. I think about it. "Actually I guess I'm not. This is just the way it is."

She gets in and kneels. She's hugging herself and shivering. "Don't you have a heater?" she says. "I'm going to run my nylons."

"No." I get out and start peeling the covering off the car. It used to be red, now it's white.

"What are you doing?" she says when I get back in. She has my sleeping bag wrapped around her shoulders.

"Molting. Now we're camouflaged."

She hangs on to the metal dash and the doorhandle. We bounce over the rutted ice and frozen mud.

"How far are you going?"

"Los Angeles."

"On this road?"

I shrug. She's wearing a polyester suit with a skirt. She even has a little tie-like thing on. I look back over my shoulder to see what kind of shoes she's wearing. Light-duty nylon hiking boots.

She sees me look and says, "I left my high-heels in the car. I know this looks ridiculous."

"Yeah." I guess her underwear is probably made of nylon too. Spandex maybe. I look at her face. Maybe her make-up is made of petroleum too. She glances over and catches my eye. She has a strained smile, she winces on the bumps.

"Watch the road," she says.

"I'm turning here. To the right."

She looks out the window. "Is this the road to Snakeyes Ranch?"

"I guess. I'm turning off before that."

"So am I," she says.

The road is a one-lane driveway of two wheelruts like the Oregon Trail. It winds through the snowy woods for a couple of miles. There's only a few inches of new snow since the last fourwheel-drive rig went through. I jack us up a couple inches more and the woman gasps and grabs the metal dashboard with her white knuckles. We bounce and slide along the rutted track. The craters and divots are softened by the snow.

"What kind of car is this?" she says.

"A one-off."

"Oh." With one hand she clutches the sleeping bag like a swollen shawl. "This is a warm sleeping bag," she says. "Do you think we'll get stuck?"

I don't say anything. I make myself think of something else. After all how I feel depends on what I think about. And what I think about is up to me. I need to keep myself pure. There's a point to all this. I'm not some victim of random spasms. I don't suffer from sexual convulsions. I make myself think of something other than what her underwear is made of. She's just trying to rob my attention from me. If I lose that

I've got nothing.

I take the turn-off to Goat's place and skid down the rough track. She's headed there too. We pull up by his six-sided log cabin. It's built of old telephone poles. The creosote is all leeched out of them and they make fine logs. He still hasn't finished the second story. He hasn't started it. Maybe the one story is enough. We get out and the goats flock over and jump up on the car, leaving muddy hoof-prints.

"Get off!" she shouts at them, waving her arm. Her other arm clutches her big flat purse. The goats stare at her. "They'll scratch your paint."

Goat comes out wearing a thick wool mackinaw. His breath makes clouds. He squints at us from behind his furry blond beard. "You again," he says, looking at her.

"That's right," she says. Her mouth is a thin little white line.

"Reinforcements, huh," he says squinting up at me. His glance catches on me. "Don't I know you?"

"Sure."

"I presume she's still in the same place," says the woman in oil. I see now that it's a vinyl briefcase tucked under her arm. She pulls on a pair of fake-leather gloves.

"Nope," says Goat.

"What? Where is she?"

"Gone."

"Gone where?"

He shrugs. "Just walked out, into the snow."

"What do you mean, just walked out?"

"You know, like the Eskimos, you lie down in a blizzard, everything goes all numb and peaceful-like."

"What!"

"Guess the heat just got too intense, you know?"

"What about the child."

He shrugs. "Went along for the ride I guess."

"God damn it," she says. She paces back and forth and starts to open her little vinyl briefcase and snaps it shut again. "I just can't wait to write this one up. I've had it up to here with you, you nuts and your pseudo-Indian crap. Up to here!" She stomps around in a little circle. "Up to here," she says, flinging her arm way up. "When was all this?"

"I don't know, a few weeks. Last big snow, when was it?"

"This was an open-and-shut case. Damned bureaucracy. Wait till they see my report, their ears will burn! Of course I'll have to go make an inspection."

"Suit yourself."

She looks off toward the woods, downslope. "Which way was it now?"

He points. "Down through there. When you hit the second gully follow it down."

"Uh, right. I think I remember."

"It's only a half-mile or so once you hit the gully. Can't miss it."

She nods and stalks off through the snow.

"If you get lost again just follow your tracks back," he calls after her. "Ain't you going with her?" he says squinting at me.

"Who were you talking about?"

"I don't know, when?"

"Walking off into the snow and lying down and going to sleep?"

"Aw, just somebody from around here. Ain't you with her?"

"Her car was stuck in the ditch and I gave her a lift. That's not Paledawn you were talking about," I say with a rock in my

14

gut. My vision is blurring at the edges and narrowing to a thin vertical focus. All I see is Goat's face, stretched and elongated. The tufty beard makes him look like a goat-devil. He grins.

"Was it?" I shout.

"Oh yeah, I remember you. Her brother."

I grab him by the front of his mackinaw and shake him. "God damn it!" I shout.

"Relax, it's ok." He glances back over his shoulder, downslope. "She's all right. It's a hoax."

I let go. He grins. "A big put-on, man. Don't you know who that lady is?"

"What lady?"

He nods over his shoulder, after the fresh tracks. "Child Protection Agency. She came up here a month or two ago, said they heard about a woman with a baby living on less than 500 bucks a year."

"So what business is it of theirs?"

"Man they make it their business. They're getting paid to do stuff, you know. They get in trouble if they're just sitting in their offices all day. She said 500 bucks was below the federal subsistence level and they'd have to check on putting the kid in a foster home. Paledawn's gone underground. So if we pull it off they'll write her off. Maybe they'll delete her social security number. She's free, man." He laughs.

He points out a faint track in the snow cutting across the gentle slope to the north. "You can leave your car here but the goats'll thrash the paint. If they haven't already. Sorry."

"It's ok, there's plenty more under that."

I leave the car and trudge through the snow. Fresh footprints cross the faint track and lead uphill. The prints are tiretread soles like Paledawn uses on her homemade boots. I wind up through the pines and skirt around a short cliff. I hear a whoop from above and glance up. Paledawn stands holding a huge bundle of deadwood in one arm, grinning down at me. She stands sideways in her long wool cape made from a Hudson Bay Company blanket. I can see Indigo's rosy red face grinning out at me from inside the tiny cloth tent where she's strapped tight against her mother's back.

Paledawn leads me farther upslope toward her place. Indigo is too little to remember me but she grins quietly at me all the way. She twists to look back at me if I drop behind. She keeps me in sight. They don't get much company, maybe she does remember me. Their old place down the ravine, where they lived the last time I came, was a round hut about five yards across, dug two feet into the ground with a wall of vertical boards and a sod roof. It took Paledawn a month to build and the day she finished chinking the walls was the day she went into labor. They lived there a few years, till now.

We come to a tiny canvas wickiup, a dozen feet across and five feet high at the top of the dome. A bent stovepipe sticks out the top. Paledawn throws a flap open and we crawl in. It feels bigger inside than it looks from outside.

She says, "When I built our round house I carried everything I owned to the spot in one load. When we decided to leave we had all kinds of stuff. Since there's two of us now I carried two loads. Indigo helped pick what to bring."

"My dollie," she says, smiling and hugging it. It's a carved wooden doll dressed in homemade Indian clothes.

Paledawn lights a fire in the tiny sheetmetal stove. "It's much better here. I could always feel the weight of that sod roof, pressing down. This is so much lighter."

"Won't blow away will it?"

She smiles. "Not here in the trees." We crowd in close to the stove and the warmth washes over us. "When the sun

16

comes out we roll up the walls and let the breeze blow through. And we don't need so much wood, heating all that space. That place was a fortress! I didn't come here to live inside. I came here to live under the sky."

She tells me I'm lucky, there's a party that night. At Chikory's and her mate's. Chikory is the midwife who helped deliver Indigo. Now she's eight months pregnant and she's been having a rough time. I ask if she ever went to see a doctor.

"Naw we don't go for that crap, we're mountain people, we take care of our own."

"I don't know, if I broke my leg or something I think I'd want to have a doctor take a look at it."

"Indigo's never been to a doctor and she's a perfectly healthy little girl. Aren't you Indigo."

"Aren't I what, Paled'n?"

"In college when I got an abortion I had to go to Canada, it cost 500 dollars. This spring I gave myself a herbal abortion with plants I picked here in the mountains."

"I'm glad you know what you're doing. Gawd, let's talk about something else."

"You hear anything from Ursula?"

"I was afraid that was coming up."

"What about the twins?"

"I try not to think about it much." She just looks at me. The twins. I'll die right here and now if I think about it. I've tried being dead, didn't like it much. "What am I supposed to do? There's a standing warrant out for my arrest. She'd turn me in as fast as she could dial 911." Paledawn just looks at me. "They wouldn't know me from Adam," I say.

"Do you want to know where they are?"

"What?"

"California," she says. "Orange County."

"I'm on my way to California now."

"So you did know where they are."

"Well, no. I just have this idea of showing all the people down there, the way it can be."

"Maybe you thought that was your reason for going."

"I'm in charge here," I say. "There's no hidden driver." She laughs and I ask her, "How do you know where my boys are?"

"The grapevine. Ursula's picture showed up in a magazine. Somebody passed it along to me. Somebody else tracked her down for me."

"What grapevine?"

"Never mind. They didn't say where in Orange County. Do you know where Orange County is? They acted like it was something people knew."

"It's where Disneyland is."

"Ah."

"It's near the vortex," I say. "The center of the world."

We stop to pick up Bear on the way to the party. I drive, Paledawn sits perched on my cooler with Indigo in her lap. She points the way through a labyrinth of narrow snowy tracks through black forest. We stop at a nondescript spot in the woods.

"This way," she says.

"I'll carry Indigo."

"It's not far, she can walk."

We walk slowly through the trees and up a slope. Paledawn pauses at intervals, whoops, then waits and listens. The woods darken with dusk and the air is still. Light snow falls. I walk third behind Indigo, at her pace. We catch up when Paledawn pauses to whoop and listen.

"You have to make lots of noise when you're coming to

Bear's," she says after pausing to listen. "He has a machine gun."

"What for?"

"Helicopters."

Finally a whoop comes back to us through the trees. We climb a little farther and wait. I look up the slope. Cliffs jut up out of the snow and in one of them a slab of rock swings open and a hunched hairy man comes out. He closes the cliff after him.

"Is that where he lives?"

"In a cave," she says.

He comes lumbering down the slope through the snow. He's got a rolling walk with his shoulders hunched and his arms hanging loose. He wears a big bearskin cape that hangs down past his knees and a bearskin hat and bearskin boots that disappear up under the cape. His long tangled hair and beard are nearly black and they blend in with the fur of the bear. He pulls up beside us and Paledawn introduces me and he nods, grinning. He doesn't speak or offer his hand to shake. He's short and wide. He stands peering up at me with his head to one side, grinning and nodding, his shoulders hunched and his bare arms hanging out through holes in the furry cape. The black hair on his arms is almost as thick as fur. We turn and start down and he lifts Indigo from behind. He twirls her in the air like the rotors of a helicopter and she shrieks, laughing. He sets her on his shoulders and gallops down the slope. His pumping legs make the snow fly and they gallop ahead. The little girl's laughing comes like music back through the quiet trees long after they're out of sight.

We park next to a scarred Volkswagen and two pickup trucks and we follow a dim light through the woods to a small farmhouse. We go in without knocking. People sit and lounge in the faint light of kerosene lamps. It doesn't feel like a party. Then we hear sounds from behind the door in the next room.

"Somebody hurts," says Indigo.

"It's Chikory," a woman tells Paledawn. "Been going on for hours."

Paledawn goes in through the door. I stay out in the main room with Indigo. Bear sits silently in a corner. Three people leave quietly. The dull moans and sharp cries keep on from beyond the door.

"She's having a baby," says Indigo. She looks at the door with her eyes big.

I find a guitar and play quiet for her. I make up a song about ditching the four cops. Pretty soon she's laughing and clapping and singing along with the chorus. We sing on and on. Almost everybody else quietly leaves. I play her a soft song about how it feels to go beyond 200 on the freeway. That floating feeling. It doesn't feel fast any more. You're way beyond speed. She doesn't have a clue. She's never seen a freeway. But the sound of it soothes her. She falls asleep curled in the big overstuffed chair. I lean the guitar against the chair and Bear comes and softly drapes a crocheted blanket over her. He tucks it in around her. He smiles down at her through his woolly beard.

I go looking for the bathroom and find a white kitchen instead. The light in here is bright and electric and harsh. It scorches my eyes for a second till I'm used to it. There's a young woman heating water in huge tubs on the electric stove.

"How come they always want boiled water when a baby's being born?" I ask her.

She smiles. She has a big bald spot on the side of her head.

Everywhere else her hair is long and brown and wavy. "I don't know," she says. "To wash everything with sterile water, I guess. Do I know you?"

"I'm Paledawn's brother."

"I'm Patches. See?" She lowers her head so I can see the bald area on the top and side of her head better. "I was trying to fix a tractor and my hair got in the fanbelt." She tosses her hair back. "It's starting to grow back in."

Paledawn comes in and asks where the hell Paul is. Patches doesn't know. She says Noname has gone looking for him. I follow Paledawn back into the bedroom.

It's warm and dimly lit with kerosene lamps. Chikory is naked on the bed on her knees and elbows with her face plastered against the rumpled sheet. The topsheet and the other blankets lie twisted and shoved off onto the floor. She's moaning and shaking. The midwife is thin, in her forties or fifties. She has streaks of white in her long dark hair. She's holding Chikory and asking if she can push any harder. Chikory cries out, shaking her head.

A handsome man with a trimmed beard hurries in.

"Where've you been?" Paledawn asks him, glaring.

"I just heard about it. We had a power failure, the plants were freezing. How's it going?" He glances to the midwife. She looks up. Her face doesn't say anything. He glances to Paledawn.

"It's a hard one," she says.

"What can I do?" he says.

Chikory cries out, over and over. I can't make out what it means. "She wants you to hold her," says the midwife quietly.

"Right," he nods and hurries to the bedside. He awkwardly tries to hold her from the side.

21

I crouch alongside him and keep my voice real low. "Listen, I got a car out there, we could get her down to a hospital real quick."

He shakes his head. "We're mountain people," he says softly. "She's strong."

She moans, then breaks into quick panting like a winded dog. The midwife talks to her, helping her slow it down.

"She can do it," he says. He leans toward her. "You'll be ok, won't you?"

"Over, over," she gasps.

"Here, help turn her," says the midwife. We all help turn her around. Now she's squatting propped up against the wall over the headboard. Her face is a taut grimace with her eyes squeezed hard shut. Sweat or tears soak her face. Paul holds her from one side, the midwife from the other. "Now, push!" says the midwife in a low strong voice.

She makes a sound between a groan and a scream and she bears down with her fists and teeth clenched. I expect her teeth to break any second. A slick patch of hair appears between her legs. She pauses and gasps and the midwife says "Now!" and she pushes again, screaming this time and a tiny head oozes out. On the next push the whole tiny purple body spurts out, trailing slime and the bloody cord. The midwife snatches up the baby and Chikory collapses sideways against Paul and he and Paledawn and I sit back, grinning. He strokes his wife's soaked hair and murmurs to her.

"Give me a blanket," snaps the midwife.

"Is it a boy or a girl?" says Paul.

"Give me a damned blanket!"

Paledawn hands her one and she rips open the front of her own shirt and holds the baby against her chest, and wraps the blanket around both of them.

"How come it's not crying?" says Paul.

"Get me a hot water bottle."

Paledawn hurries toward the kitchen.

"She's a girl," says the midwife. "We got to keep her warm."

"There's an electric blanket in the other bedroom," says Paul.

"Get it." He eases Chikory onto the bed and covers her with a blanket and leaves. Paledawn comes in with a hot water bottle. The midwife holds it against the side of her face and flings it aside. "Too damned hot."

"Where's my baby?" moans Chikory. Paledawn lies on the bed with her and holds her and murmurs to her softly. I'm not listening.

Paul comes in with the electric blanket and hands it to the midwife. He plugs in the cord and turns the amberlit dial up half-way. The midwife wraps the tiny baby in the blanket and dials the heat up to 10. The tiny breaths are coming fitfully and she lays the baby on the bed next to Chikory and she and Paul and I sit back and Chikory shifts over to put her arm around the baby. Then the baby's uneven breathing stops and the midwife snatches her up. She glances around quickly, holding the baby in both hands. I take it from her gently, and lean over and put my mouth over the tiny mouth and nose. The skin is warm and sticky and ever so soft. I breathe out with the softest, tiny breath. I can feel the tiny baby swell with the air. I breathe again and again. I have to remember to use the gentlest tiny breaths.

Chikory keeps calling out but I don't hear much of it. They're trying to calm her. I keep breathing. I taste the salt where my tears are running down and smearing on the baby's face. Her face feels colder each time my lips touch her smooth skin. The warmth is all coming from the hot electric blanket now. I place my mouth over hers to breathe out again and the breath is sucked out of me suddenly, making me gasp. I breathe in sharply and something catches in my throat, choking me. I start to reel backward and Paul takes the baby and I fall to my hands and knees on the floor. I gasp and cough and fight to keep from retching. I struggle to get up and stagger toward the door, stumble out into the main room and sprawl on an old couch, choking, trying to breathe, hyperventilating when I can. I black out but only for a moment, I think.

I look up and I can breathe easier and the room looks different, somehow. I don't know what it is. Every edge has a crystal sharpness to it, like I'm seeing it for the first time, or after a long bout of blindness. Like seeing it with new eyes. Like the ethereal clarity you get at 200+, almost.

Paul is coming from the bedroom. Tears run down his cheeks into his trimmed beard. I see every whisker, every tear, everything. He's holding the baby wrapped in the electric blanket against his chest. I feel an odd detachment from the dead little body, it seems like months or years since I pressed my mouth over the small red face. I have that impersonal feeling you can sometimes get toward the body where someone doesn't live any more. The heater control box trails behind Paul dangling from its cord, dragging on the floor and banging against the furniture as he goes.

I lie on the couch until Chikory starts calling out for her baby. I get up and go outside and trip over the shovel lying on the front steps. Paul sits on the steps holding the body. Bear sits beside him. They sit still and the slow snow is turning the three of them gradually white.

Paul stands up, then Bear. I pick up the shovel and follow

them into the woods. I don't know if he's looking for a special spot. We walk until he stops. I start digging. On top the ground is frozen but it's softer below. Bear takes the shovel and digs. Then Paul digs. He lays the baby in. It isn't a very big hole.

Bear carries Indigo out to the car. I have my arm around Paledawn. She's crying quietly. We start driving.

"It's so cold in here," says Paledawn. Bear drapes the sleeping bag tenderly around her shoulders from behind. "I hope I wasn't too hard on Paul," she says. "There's a certain tension, you know?"

"Yeah."

"He wanted me for his mate. It's made a strain between Chikory and me. Indigo really loves him, like a dad. I don't know, maybe I should've."

"You don't love him though."

"Oh it's not that. I don't know. Just the paranoia, the constant suspicion. He says he doesn't carry a gun."

"A gun."

"Paul's the biggest grower in the county. He makes over a hundred thousand a year."

"Yeah?"

"You see how he's trimmed his beard? And the haircut? You can tell who's growing, the more money they make the straighter they try to look." She glances back, and smiles. "Except for Bear."

I glance back. He's watching us, maybe smiling in the faint dark.

"How can he grow so much with the short summers up here?"

"He grows year-round. He gets all the men together, first big snowstorm that closes the roads they go out at night with

25

a backhoe and dig a big trench beside the county road. They cover it over and tap into the powerlines for the heaters and growlights. By morning the snow's covered all the evidence. Paul's a leader. Best businessman around here." She laughs suddenly. "Mom and Dad thought it was another example of me flaking out, that I didn't go for him. They thought he was so together. There's no way they could know I guess."

"I don't think I'd tell 'em."

"I can live with the rap. But I can't live with the scrutiny. Whether it's real or not. The paranoia."

"What do you mean, doesn't everyone live with it? I mean, everyone everywhere."

"That's not why I came out here."

I laugh. "To get rich and re-enact Vietnam."

"Right. Some of these guys have whole arsenals of stuff swiped from national guard armories."

"Concord Bridge."

"I've got something else in mind for Indigo and me," she says.

We drop Bear off beside the road. He lumbers off into the dark woods. We drive back to Goat's and I say good-bye. I hug them both. I start missing them before I've even left. I just can't slow down. The vortex is tugging on me. On something deep in me. In my chest, or my guts, or the base of my brain. Or all three.

We're sucked south with a force like gravity. For a while we take 97, needing no sleep. At dawn we turn off to head south through the Horse Heaven Hills. We have to pass through the Horse Heaven Hills, just because they're called that. We look for horses. Don't see any but we can feel them. Their gliding stride. Foamed necks stretching ahead and untrimmed manes flying. The way horses fly and their

26

hooves never touch the ground. Beside us, pacing us, 120, 130. A cop passes going the other way. We step on it and never see him again.

This is like a homecoming. It was on vacant freeways in this desert just east of the mountains that Atticus and I learned about the world of 200-plus. The purity of it. The rightness, the realness. The long level causeway from just past Vantage to Moses Lake. It starts near the town of George. Blink and you'll miss it. "If you lived in George, Washington, you'd be home now." We blinked and missed it.

The concrete is smooth and hard and level as a runway. Nothing else exists. The blur slows down and clocks don't move. Maybe they start jerking backwards. Atticus said, "This is it. It's everything." I said, "No. It can't end here. We discovered it, now we got to give it away. We can't be hoarding it. We got to take it to Rome." To where every road leads. To where all the people live distracted, with their attention scattered and stolen. They need to be shown a thing or two. Shake 'em up. They live their whole lives without a glimmering of the possibilities. They think life is a financial transaction or something. Like, how much equity you got? What's your net worth? But I say, What are you made of? That's the real question. Are you heavy or light? Are you moving or dead? And if you're moving, how fast?

After all, America's the land of the free. If you don't live that way you're not really an American. If you've got something precious you have to spread it around. Sometimes you might come off like a fanatic. Too bad. You got to be adamant. You got to be obsessed. What good is your life if you're not obsessed? You got to be pure. You're only pure if you operate on truth. Truth means you have to be right. "Yes, but." You heard that lately? Screw that! Only one thing matters. Be right. Nothing else. No matter what. Because consequences are important only if you're a wimp. Ask Atticus. Well, sorry. You can't ask Atticus. He's not here.

We cross the Columbia on a long bridge and we cross a freeway on a short one. A paltry freeway, two lanes each way. Why bother? We're headed for Mecca where two lanes each way doesn't even make a boulevard. The freeway we cross is straight and empty and we could have hit 200 easy. But it's pathetic. Two skinny lanes snaking across the country. Why do you think I had to leave Seattle? This whole part of the country is the sticks when it comes to freeways. In Seattle you got one going up and down and one shooting off to the right. A few loops and swirls thrown in. Never more than four lanes each way. I want to go 200 and stay there. I want to live there. I got a tank that holds enough alcohol to run for ten hours straight. At 200 miles an hour you burn up the freeways in Seattle in a couple of minutes. I need the sweep and the grace and the hum that swells to a roar. I need to blast. This paltry freeway runs east or west, like a frontier that needs crossing. It's just out to distract you, to rob your attention. We fly over it on the overpass. Like a horse with wings. We never pause. We're sucked south. It pulls us down like gravity.

Stronger than gravity. Because gravity is only one force and now I'm being pulled by two. I'm rushing toward the center of the known world to share a dream, and to find one. The twins. Wouldn't you know Ursula would go there, as close to the center as she can get. It's physics. The vacuum inside her pulls her around. I used to be that way. I remember the feeling. Now, sometimes, I feel too full. So full it catches in my throat and I can hardly breathe. It happens every time I start to slow down.

In Oregon 395 crosses broad open valleys in straight lines

and sweeping curves. Then it winds and twists over the snowy forested ridges between them. In the valleys the ranches are covered with gray-white old snow that reflects the sky. The snowplows have piled it on the shoulders. The snow makes low borders and the road is a wide shallow trench. We slide down it toward California. The frost heaves in the broken pavement are levelled by the snow into smooth humps. They launch us and we fly airborne for dozens of yards before gliding down soft in a cloud of ice-dust.

Over the low passes the plowed snow on the shoulders makes walls and we twist up and over. It's like following a toboggan track in the Olympics on TV. Only better because this isn't TV. I roll down the window so the thin frozen air blasts in. I stick my head out so I'm not looking through glass.

We stop to rest on one of the low passes and start south again in pitch dark. We barrel down the winding toboggan chute lit by our stark swivelling headlights. The earth flattens and we fly through rangeland. High deserted desert with tufts of sage and tumbleweed breaking the wide wind-rolled snowy country.

The towns are still and barely lit. The road is abandoned and we can go as fast as we want. I keep it in check. This is still the sticks. It's only a warm-up. Nothing matters here. We're on a collision course with the bigtime.

Sometimes I feel like the last survivor of a dying race. The next second I feel like the first man of a new one. Stand up, take a few deep breaths and look around with new eyes. It doesn't make sense but I don't expect it to. Sometimes the only time things make sense is when it would make more sense for them not to.

Even way out in the sticks they have border crossings

coming into California. They pretend it's about fruit. Right.
I really believe them. Who can submit to that kind of
inquisition? The bureaucracy, the red tape. "Got any fruit?"
"None of your fuckin' business, asshole." Sorry. It's just not
right. We don't submit. We drive past at something over a
hundred. We crank it up to 140 for twenty minutes. Then I
pull over and peel the white off the car. Won't be needing the
snow camouflage. The goats had nicked it up anyway. Now
the car is blue. I take off the New Hampshire plates and stash
them inside. You can't throw away plates that say "Live Free
or Die." I mount a set of Yukon Territory plates, red and
white. They got so few cars there they only need a few
numbers. The rest of the space is taken up by the figure of a
prospector panning for gold.

We get back on the road and keep it down to sixty. A few
minutes later two gestapo cars go blazing past with their blue
lights flashing. They think 110 is fast. We never see them
again. Maybe they get sucked clear on down to Los Angeles
too.

The light is fading when we fly up the gentle grade toward
the lip of Redrock Canyon. An old Wagoneer is stopped on
the shoulder with the hood up. We blur past an old woman
standing by the car. I touch the brakes. They've hardly ever
been used. We swerve a little and screech to a stop. I spin
around, backtrack, spin around again and stop in front of her
car.

She wants a lift. I give her one. Her face is covered with tiny
cracks. I drag the toolbox forward and throw my folded
sleeping bag over it for her to sit on. We barrel down the line
for a few minutes and then she wants to head out to the left
on a dirt track.

"Let me out," she says. "It's not far to my place, maybe

someone'll come along."

"I'll take you."

"This rig ain't built for it. You'll bottom out."

I raise the suspension, hydraulically.

"Wow," she says. "Slick."

We bounce across the desert into the El Paso Mountains. She curses her car. She's going to leave it there. She's an army nurse, retired. She lives in a shack on the side of a mountain just below Burro Schmidt's Mine.

"You can stop and see my museum," she says. "No donation required. I'll loan you a miner's kerosene lamp for walking through the mine. Ever heard of Burro Schmidt?"

I haven't.

"Came out in 1901 from Providence. They said he was dying of consumption."

"Consumption. I'd say we all are."

"Hah!" she snorts. "They told him he had exactly six months to live. Not a day longer. He's in the Ripley's Believe It Or Not. The Human Mole. You sure you never heard of him?"

"Keep reminding me. Maybe it'll come back to me."

"Started his own gold mine. They were hitting paydirt all through these mountains. So he started digging. Dug that shaft every day for forty years. Dug clear through the mountain till he was about to break out on the far side, and made a hard left turn. Dug straight off that way till he almost busted through to the north. Went back to the junction and dug south and finally broke through with that shaft. Miscalculated, I figure. Never found nothing."

I don't say anything.

"What do you think of that?" she says.

"Makes you wonder how he felt when he busted through."

31

She squints at me, deepening the cracks that crisscross her face. "Don't you wonder why he did it in the first place?"

"Did what?"

"All that digging."

I shrug. "Makes sense to me."

"It does?"

"Sure."

"What do you mean it makes sense?"

"It just does."

She watches me. "Huh."

"It seems American."

"The shaft takes a lot of upkeep," she says. "Maybe you'd like to stay on, help out."

"No thanks."

"I can pay. Not much, but a little."

"I got to keep moving. It's like gravity."

I drop her off and turn around. She lives in an old trailer high on the shoulder of one of the biggest mountains. Beside her trailer stands Schmidt's tiny shack. It's her museum now. "Crammed with junk I found all through these mountains," she says. "Used to be lots of people up here, now it's empty except when the city folks bring their dirtbikes up on weekends." The mine is up a dirt track just around the bend. She invites me again to stay a while, just to take a tour around and look in the mine. "Nearly a mile long, clear through the mountain," she says. Sure, it sounds interesting. I'd take a look if I had the time. But who has the time? And the thought of that long, darkening tunnel, maybe constricting as you go in deeper and deeper—something catches in my throat, making it hard to breathe. I mean it sounds great, lady, but it took the guy what, forty years? To go less than a mile? Screw that. It's just not fast enough. We have to get going. We're

32

miles and miles of rutted desert road from 395. We're farther from where we have to be, not closer. We're slowing down when we should be accelerating.

There are five theories about what will happen when we reach Los Angeles.

We might be repelled and bounced back into the desert. By something operating at the atomic level, like opposite poles on magnets. If this is it we've got to hit the forcefield with the greatest possible momentum. That's how you get hurled back with the most blinding speed.

We might pass through and career off at greater acceleration than we had coming in. Like a satellite that comes tumbling toward Earth at a tangent and gets slingshotted off into outer space. The nearer your arc passes to the center the faster the whiplash snaps you out and beyond. Assuming you don't come too close and end up splattered against one of the taller trees or mountain peaks or skyscrapers. Initial speed is vital because the hotter you come in the hotter you go out.

Or we might be sucked in with the overpowering gravity of a giant black hole. Sucked in and crushed into a mass packed so tight a teaspoon weighs ten thousand pounds. If this is it you got to come in as fast as you can. Get everything blurred to where it freezes to a standstill. If you reach the speed of light maybe time starts turning backward. Even the all-time greatest screw-ups might be reversible. At the very least you could unravel them a little. Or maybe at the speed of light we'll just plain disappear.

Or maybe when we hit L.A. nothing will happen. It's happened before.

It's dark when we reach the main highway. I stop in the scrub just out of the headlit illumination of the cars and trucks and motor homes droning past. I peel off the blue layer and we're red again.

I lift the trunk lid. The whole thing is filled with the fuel tank. I dip it. Almost half full.

Los Angeles will be the place to fill it. There's sure to be some industrial joint that sells bulk alcohol. Without connections it's almost impossible to get it in the sticks. There's plenty out there but if you're not local nobody's going to admit they even know what a still is. If they haven't known you all your life they're sure you're a federal agent. You can get killed asking about pure grain alcohol in small towns and country gas stations.

You can always disconnect the pre-ignition device and adjust the timing and run gas through your engine. I'd rather shoot myself. On alcohol you run your engine 25,000 miles between oil changes. It comes out as clean and clear and honey-tinted as the day you poured it in. Gas is so filthy it's a sacrilege. It would be torment to know the gritty black soot was working past my rings and scoring my cylinder walls. Polluting my golden oil and grating under my bearings and grinding on my shaft. Eating my engine from the inside out, mile by gliding mile.

It's cold in the desert and I get in the car and wrap the sleeping bag around my shoulders. It almost would've been worth it to put in a heater. But who needs the clutter. It's distracting. We need clarity. We don't need robbers of attention. And we're almost to Los Angeles and we'll never think about a heater again. We'll be plenty warm just from the friction of passing through the air at blazing speeds. Friction can burn a shooting star to pure ash. Maybe it'll do the same to us. That's the fifth theory.

We crest the rise at the lip of the canyon and see far ahead the lights of Los Angeles spread out before us. Glittering and sparkling in the clear desert air. I didn't realize we were so close. But that air magnifies things and maybe we're not so close after all. It doesn't matter. When we get there, we'll be ready.

I accelerate going down the canyon and blast through the sweeping curves. Corrugated cliffs loom and swing past at the headlights' edge. You have to keep accelerating as you near the vortex. That vast sprawl of lights could thrill and mesmerize you and sear your focus. Awe and expectation and dread and desire suck us onward, faster and faster. If you pause, your momentum can reverse on you. It hurls you ricocheting back, spinning looping and wobbling into an unstable orbit that can land you anywhere but where you want to get: the center of the Universe.

We hit the flats and bomb across. I don't bother checking the speedometer. My eyes are fixed on the dazzle of lights spread across the level horizon ahead. We blur past miles of sage and tumbleweed at the borders of light along the roadside. Los Angeles is about to rise up out of the desert dead ahead. The lights are invisible behind a low rise but their glow lights up the sky. We crest and slow, curving into a town. Mojave. We haven't reached L.A. yet. Up close the lights are more scattered. They're not so bright. From back there the shimmering sparkle seemed to spread out endlessly. Now you can see how paltry the joint was. The desert air had blown it all out of proportion. It's a hick town where another highway joins ours. That's the extent of it. The stoplights and traffic slow us down through the strip town. Passing is going to be tougher from here on in.

There are no qualms in the car. There are no doubters. No cynics. We create our own false expectations. We'll be ready when we find Los Angeles. Or when she finds us. You got to laugh it off and hold your focus. All right, it was only Mojave. Ha ha, we got tricked. Big deal. You have to believe your beliefs. When the Muslims catch an infidel trying to sneak into Mecca they stone him to death. It's no different in Los Angeles. Unbelievers are shot on the freeway.

Just out of town the highway branches into a little freeway. Two lanes each way. A little capillary flowing inward. Plugged into the whole throbbing pulsating network. Sucking us inward, toward the heart.

The traffic is spread out on our two ingoing lanes and the passing is easy at well over a hundred. Now we're getting a taste of reality. It can only get better, when the freeways get thicker and the suction pulls stronger and faster the closer you come to the heart.

The next rise brings us into a whistle-stop called Rosamond. This is historic. Ahead lies our first true glimpse of the city. At last. Whole galaxies of vibrating lights splatter clear across the horizon. We whistle through a buffeting west wind. The freeway leads straight and true and flat. I can't believe it's still only two lanes, here on the brink of the bigtime. We begin to pass through the outermost lights. The whole schematic of light stretches out toward us and envelops us and we're not in a city at all. Just a long scattering of lights. Thousands of lights scattered across the desert. There are no signs for Los Angeles. We're not there yet. We're not even close. The thickest the lights get are at two little towns called Lancaster and Palmdale. Two more places I never heard of before.

How can you be sure you're really in Los Angeles when you finally get there? A double-walled fortress defended on all sides by false cities. Rogue cities. Ghost-L.A.s with the real city hiding somewhere behind a screen of deceptor-cities.

How many people come aiming for the center, only to bounce off? Or bog down and get shunted off to some secondary satellite city. Stuck on the periphery of what's really real. Exiled to a frontier town.

But it's right in a way. It makes sense. Of course it wouldn't be hanging right out in the open for any casual nerd to yank on. Real truth and true beauty don't operate that way. They lie concealed. Hidden away for the few, for those of us who know what we're looking for. Who know where it is and what it's for. That's how purity operates. Nothing's so clear-cut. You have to dream it first. Then maybe—maybe—you'll know it when you see it.

We fly through dark canyons and up hills and down. Our freeway is three lanes now. In the distance we begin to see scatterings of light. Promising, maybe even seductive. But we won't be fooled again. Straight on then. We'll know when we know, and not before. I feel more urgency than ever before. Desperate almost. I feel a tightness in my chest and throat, almost a choking. I have to fight it down. I have to try to think about something else and push down a little harder on the gas.

Finally coming down an endless grade we merge with a four-laner feeding the city. We're six lanes each way now and together we make twelve. The cars and trucks slide roaring down and forward and below us spread all the billions of twinkling lights of the city. Well, maybe not. I'm not making any assumptions but what else could it be? Twelve lanes more or less, who's counting? We're in the thick of it now. Blasting across the flats, crossing and ducking under wide freeways with names I've never heard of—five lanes each way to someplace called the Simi Valley! Incredible. This has to be it.

Only it isn't. The green overhead freeway signs are still pointing out the lanes to take to get to Los Angeles. Five lanes feed that way. We're not there yet. I cross over just in time to catch the freeway leading onward, inward. We were nearly shunted off onto some other route. There's no going back on a freeway. It's always one-way. The signs only tell you which exits lie up ahead. They never say a word about the ones you passed. You keep blasting onward, inward, and the chances are good that you'll never pass the same interchange twice.

I've never been crossed up on a freeway in my life. I came this close just now. It rattles me. I step down on the throttle, to ease back up toward 90 and settle my nerves. There are so many cars. We can't get it up to 90, even with lane-changes. They keep clogging things up, ahead, behind, to either side. It's sometime in the middle of the night and the jerks are clogging up the freeway! We're pinned in, held down to 65 and 70. Only an occasional burst toward 80. Then, boxed in again. Swerving, switching lanes, twisting your neck off.

What the hell is this? It's not supposed to be like this. We keep following the wide green signs for Los Angeles. We start up a grade and the whole freeway is slowing down. We can't have this, anything is better. We'll scream down the shoulder. I work over to the fast lane but there's no shoulder. You can see where they moved the lanelines over, gobbling up the inside shoulder and narrowing the widths and getting an extra lane out of it without widening the pavement.

What is this chintzy shit? This is the world capital of freeways, what the hell do they think they're doing penny-pinching on one miserable lane? This isn't what we came here for. There's no hitting 200 on this assembly line. Christ. It must be rush-hour. My sense of timing must be screwed up. I've been in such a hurry. I've always been but lately, more

so. Much more. There's no slowing down. Not for a second.
I guess I stopped to eat but I can't remember when, or what
I ate. I guess I slept but I can't remember sleeping. Oh well.
Life's like that sometimes. Something must have thrown my
timing off. It has to be rush-hour. Bad timing. I've always had
the greatest sense of timing. Naturally, without ever having
to think about it. I'll get it back. It's just a question of getting
in synch. We'll have to come back when the timing's right.
We'll hit this stretch sometime in the middle of the night,
when the nerds are at home in bed and we got six lanes to
weave through and wander across at gliding speeds that
bring motion almost to a state of crystalline immobility.

The freeway is slowing down again. We're under forty and
almost bumper to bumper. It feels like a standstill. The
slowest this car ever went when it wasn't speeding up from
a stop or slowing down to a stop. I can't take it. The thought
of gridlock. I swerve to the right, cutting across lanes. From
behind me comes honking and screeching. We never both-
ered to put in blinkers or brakelights, who needs that crap
when you're whistling past at a hundred miles an hour faster
than the slugs you're passing?

I angle toward the right shoulder. They haven't gobbled
up the shoulder on this side for extra lanes yet. Oh, wait'll we
come back at 2 a.m., we'll show you the blazing unleashed
potential in this clogged broad desecrated swath of concrete.
We'll set it right. We'll atone for this rush-hour obscenity and
we'll cleanse our minds and clear our eyes and pay some
homage, at 190 and beyond.

We swerve to miss the scattered pieces of a rusted tailpipe
strewn along the shoulder, then crank it up a little and fly
down the shoulder at close to 80. I feel better already. The sea
of geeks is frozen in a solid grinding mass on our left. An

endless strip of sweating and crystallized humanity. Criminals! Blasphemers! They think this is reality—until, suddenly, Who's this now, what in the hell was that, streaking past in a reddish blur down the right shoulder? You can't drive on the shoulder! It's—it's—uh, it's not fair! That's what it is. Come back here, you. Sorry, heathens. God's on my side. I'm in motion. Isn't that proof enough? Come on, join me in Paradise. What's stopping you? The WASP-Mafia cop-puppets are all jammed into the gridlock with the rest of the infidels. What are you afraid of? We can all be Jesus on the 405, or the 101, or the six-oh-whatever.

I'm laughing and letting her loose. Let her go, let her run. We hump and soar down the blacktopped shoulder, crunching over the light dusting of busted safety glass. I'm blind with speed and freedom and I miss the signs and they nail us. The shoulder goes branching off suddenly. We go with it, walled off by a solid column of the creeping dead. They're bumper to bumper with the headlights of each lighting up the insides of the car ahead, like they do in funeral processions. Gawd! No way through. We brake hard and keep veering right with the curve of the shoulder. The raised divider is between us and the freeway now. We keep braking and swerve left to try to force an opening, and have to swerve back. They stand their ground, they're unflinching. They have solidarity. It's a wall and there's no getting through. No giving way for some erratic swerving hick with no blinkers and no brakelights and license plates with drawings of some grizzled prospector panning for gold. I should've switched to California plates before hitting the bigtime. To blend in, like a chameleon. The guardrail is between us and the freeway now. There's no backing up on the freeway. That's rule number one. Not that there are any rules. But when we built the transmission we didn't bother putting in a reverse gear. Who needs the extra clutter? We aim to go ahead.

The off-ramp keeps narrowing and curving right. Finally we force an opening in the slow line and wedge our way in. We slow, and stop. We're one of them now. We wait. Wait! Does anyone know what for? We're off the freeway.

Nothing like this ever happened before. The freeway was my show, my arena. It's always been home to me. I never knew an instant of doubt or confusion or fear on the freeway. I was king. And before I was king, I was the crown prince. I was born and bred for it. I'm an American. I love the freeway.

And now it's dumped on me. We're stuck here, we're waiting. Just like all the rest. Nobody knowing what for. Waiting to die. God. Don't forget to take a number.

I screwed up. It wasn't the freeway. Grow up and face it. It's me. I'm the one who blew it. The freeway's your tabula rasa. What you going to write there? I just drew a scribbling line right off the edge of the damned page. It was up to me. I'm the one who got us into this. It's up to me to get us out.

Actually, it makes sense. Of course I blew it right off the bat like this. Here's the bigtime. Here I come, blowing in from the sticks. I'm a hick, I mean, I'm from Seattle. We got one freeway going up and down and one shooting off to the right. A few ancillary twists and swirls and feeder lines. Sure, I got a message, I got a gift. You think they want to hear about it, here in the mainstream? Come on. What the hell did you expect. Wise up, dumbshit. You're a god damn provincial. You come blowing in to the bigtime and expect to blow 'em all off the road at 200+ the first time out? And at *rush-hour?* Jesus. What's the matter with me?

We stop at many stoplights. They're machines that hang in the air and show colored lights that tell you when to stop, go and watch it. Right, stupid. We all know that. Even people in Iran know that. Never mind that they have the lights upside down over there.

OK. Only it's not so obvious. There's more to it than meets the eye. They tell you when to go, but they're not called golights. Here's why. It's about control. You can always go. Straight ahead, that's the American way. It comes to us naturally, it's an instinct we got. You don't need a light to tell you when to go. That's the default mode for an American. Always has been. Get going and keep going. We never got over the shock of running into the damned ocean. That was nearly a death-blow. We never recovered.

And then hot on its heels came stoplights. When our resistance was down. They're unnatural, like a stillbirth. All that arrested potential. Frozen possibilities. Twenty years earlier they never would've took. Stoplights were a big step backward for America. Hitting the ocean and stoplights were a one-two punch. We're still reeling. We're dazed and staggering with no guard up. They're closing in for the knockout punch. See that's what this is all about. My life I mean. Bobbing and weaving. And blasting, straight ahead. Blurring past before they can lay the glove on you. I'm in the clear out here. I slipped through the ropes and I'm not even in the ring. Out here, we fight by my rules. No gloves. You should feel what you're hitting. In fact, no rules.

It was a black day in Cleveland in 1903. They put up a stoplight. That's no surprise. Lots of stupid things have been done over the centuries. I mean, think of all the millions of people who went through life thinking God didn't want them to fuck. It's twisted. It's almost as stupid as putting up a stoplight. But it would have been tolerable, if someone just put it up. A weird footnote in history. Get this, in 1903 some nut in Ohio put up this weird tower with three lights called a stoplight.

Only it didn't stop there. This is the bad part. Don't drive on if you don't have the stomach for it. Nobody'll hold it against you. It's not easy for an American to think about the virus that feeds on the American dream. The night of the walking dead wasn't a movie, it was last night. And tonight, and tomorrow. Hopefully, not the night after that. I'm working on it. I'm working on the driving dead. Don't you think it might wake you up some, when you're doing 60 on the southbound 405 somewhere around Hawthorne or Downey and someone or something blurs past you in the fast lane somewhere on the far side of 210 miles an hour? You'll feel the heat of my wake burning your cheek as it washes over you and for the next few miles you'll take an extra glance in the mirror before changing lanes. Maybe, gradually, you'll fall back asleep. That's your problem. I won't.

What happened in Cleveland wasn't that some nut propped up the colored-light tower and plugged it in and everyone laughed and the lights burned out and it was a joke in the footnotes of history. See, somebody paid attention to it. They *minded*. Who the hell was it? The first dipshit who sat waiting at a red light when nobody was coming should have been taught to bow and shipped to Japan. He'd like doing calisthenics and singing company songs before starting work each morning. He wasn't an *American*. Don't blame it on a woman, they didn't let women drive cars in those days. It was a macho thing. And some macho dirtball sat there waiting until this light with no brain told him it was safe to cross the street. Oh my God! It just doesn't make sense. I've never waited at a red light when nobody's coming. I never will. It's a question of life and death. I'd choke and die. Who could breathe? Some twit with a badge and a motorcycle aiming his electric blow-dryer at you doesn't make it right either. If you can go you got to. Life isn't long enough to live any other way. If you might make it you have to try. That's the way Lewis and Clark saw it. Heroes don't go asking for guarantees and 5-year/50,000-mile warranties. And Americans are heroes. Every last one of us. It's the nature of the critter. Love it or leave it. Go back to Europe. The Old Country. Wise up and learn something about yourself. Don't you know your ancestors were miserable peasants who came here because they wanted something more out of life? So quit settling for less. God damn it, quit settling. This is America. Step on the gas. The light turned green half an hour ago.

There's another thing that actually makes sense about Los Angeles. In addition to the freeways, of course. In Los Angeles you never have to worry about sitting at a red light with no cars coming. Every street's in gridlock all the time. When the light goes green everybody finally moves and the intersection is blocked solid. Then it turns green for the other street and they block it solid the other way. I'm not saying stoplights make sense here. I'm saying you never have a realistic chance of making it across when it isn't green. Even then it's usually chancy. Anyone you might find driving in a place like Los Angeles is not to be trusted. So you look before you leap, if you have half the sense you were born with. Because stoplights are no guarantee either. Even if they were, an American wouldn't believe in them.

The freeway is off to the left but every corner has a sign saying you can't turn left. That makes sense. What they trying to do, empty half the city? Get everybody to one side? All right. We turn right. Not because there's no sign saying you can't. Signs are made to be fucked with. Whenever I need

4 x 4s to build something I go out at night and pull up a few street signs. Actually all those no-left-turn-anytime signs make me want to turn left worse than ever. Just to show 'em. To show me, actually. Only it's physically impossible. There's a solid wall of cars coming the other way.

I see some fools turn left. They wait in the intersection with their blinkers on till the light changes. Then they trust that the idiots coming across both ways at once won't smash into them before they can scurry across. I could never do that. Not because I have no blinker (they're only good for setting people up and then doing the opposite anyway). Rather, because I could never sit straddling an intersection and pinning my survival on whether the onrushing dolts will hold off on the throttle long enough for me to squirt through.

We turn right onto a shining boulevard that stretches endlessly. A few blocks ahead a crowd of men on horseback is swarming down through the slow-going traffic toward us. They range clear across the street, weaving through the honking and braking cars. The horsemen swear and slam cars with their nightsticks and shake the sticks at drivers who yell out their windows. They're mounted cops. It's a lot like the charge of the light brigade must have been. Really been. I know, my grandmother's grandfather was there. He told her and she told me and I'll tell my grandchildren. Forget the propaganda poems and the Errol Flynn crap. You see the confusion and the foaming and frothing of the horses. You can read a horse's eyes and a horse's gait and bearing. An idiot can tell which horse will win a race before it starts. Just look at 'em. They know when something tribal is happening. They know when their side's winning and when it's losing.

The difference between here and the Crimea is that this

time it isn't the uniforms on horseback that are taking it in the shorts. This is a heavy brigade. Heaviness in the faces of the men and the withers of the horses. What are they made of to make them so heavy? What do they eat, rocky mountain oysters? The dark blue polyester outfits and the excess gear hanging from their sagging belts. The blue imitation cowboy hats with brims too narrow to do any good. No cowboy would wear a hat with so narrow a brim.

They're herding women. They're taking a heavy toll. Behind comes a police bus scooping up the women. Some people stand still and the cops wash past and beyond them. But the women in hotpants and vinyl miniskirts and meshed stockings and garish faces know they're marked and they run. They hide and run again with the terror of horses in their big black-painted eyes.

Three run together down the centerline toward us. One brown one pink and one pasty white. This isn't right. I yell out the window, "Get in!" and reach across and unlatch the door. They pile in, stumbling over no seat and over each other. They're panting and yelling. One cries. The one on the bottom. I shout to shut up and stay down. It's easy to keep low with no seats. I throw the sleeping bag over them. They huddle, moaning and shaking. I tell them again to keep quiet and I switch a lever on the dash that shuts off the open headers and routes the exhaust through a fully baffled and muffled system. The throaty farting cough of the big engine drops to a deep distant rumble. Like a rumor of artillery or distant bombing. The posse cops come, you can hear them shouting and banging the sticks and the clop of the horses' hooves on pavement. One woman whimpers and another swears and punches her under the sleeping bag, and she sobs quietly. The cops are two cars ahead, riding toward us. One car ahead. They surround us. I wait to hear the sound of one of their sticks on the car. I'll have to jump out and drag him down off his horse. Don't go hitting the car. He doesn't.

We're past. We made it. We're free. The cars move, a little. We move too. Not much. The women come out from under the sleeping bag. Their makeup is smeared all over their hideous faces.

"You saved us," says one. They're not crying any more. They look back. Nobody laughs. They're too scared. I laugh, at something else.

"Where we going?" she says.

"The freeway."

"This ain't the way."

"Maybe it's another freeway," says another.

"Which freeway?"

"Doesn't matter."

"If it don't matter how come you want to find it?"

"I want to drive 200 miles an hour down the freeway."

Nobody speaks for a while.

"Let me know when," says one. "So I can get out."

"It's fuckin' weird," says another.

The third says something I can't understand. The dark brown one.

"What's that?"

"She says she's staying, for the ride."

"Yeah?"

She says something else I can't understand.

"Says she wants to go 200 on the freeway."

They start giving me directions. I'm choking again, it's too crowded in the car. They keep looking back. I can't see what it is that's following us. I never have seen it. Finally I give up looking.

47

We're in hell. We're stuck on the surface streets. With the stoplights and the one-ways and the no-left-turns and no-U-turns and no-right-turns. It could almost make you wish you had a reverse gear. Almost. Mostly we're stuck with the gentles, the horseheads and the swines. Billions and billions of them. Streams and hordes and phalanxes of them. Rush-hour goes on and on here.

There's an attitude problem down here on the surface. I've always had trouble with surface-street people. On the free-way you can be a certain type of person. You can believe in certain things. Like purity. Like the way things ought to be. I'm only a little step beyond that. A logical step. I believe in the way things have to be. Not so with surface-street people. They grub along the ground all day with their noses too close to the dirt and the spit and the grime and the gutter. Angling and scamming for shady underhanded opportunities. Sneaking through yellow lights. Slipping in free rights and an occasional left after the light goes red. Fuck the lights. Keep your foot on the gas. Cars should be built with no brakes. There's a utopian world all right. But that doesn't appeal to surface-street people. They compromise. Calculate. Hey, there's no such thing as a calculated risk. There's risk and there's cowardice and there's nothing in between. There is no middle class. That's it. Sorry.

Sometimes we see pillars and overpasses and the promise of an upper, a smoother, a freer way. But there's no way on. Then suddenly there's an opening, widely beckoning like a concrete funnel. We swirl inward—only it turns out to be a causeway leading to an underground parking garage for a shopping mall. It sucks us down and spins us around and around, deeper down, always deeper, a swirling spiral vortex there's no getting out of. You have to resort to drastic measures, when you got no reverse gear and you can't back out the way you came in. The truth of labyrinths is that there might be no way out. It might go on forever. And if there's no minotaur it's that much worse. Because then there's no getting out, ever.

We follow a long winding tube down and down and down. There's no clue how deep, the levels are by color instead of number. I'm straining to breathe. I have that strange feeling of having been here before, not that long ago. Deja vu. We come to a fork in the tunnel. I stomp on the brake and we squeal to a stop. Momentum throws the women forward, yelling and wailing. I roll down the window, the poisonous dead air wafts in. I listen hard for any sound that might tell me which branch leads upward and out.

The echoes and reverberations of the women's wailing rattles down the corridors and clatters back to us, shattered and syncopated and exaggerated. The left path sounds clearer. I crank the wheel and slam down the gas and we peel out. The women cut loose with a new round of screaming and moaning. It bounces off the walls and baffled channels and comes back to me—I drive with my head out the window and the gas down hard, skidding the car around the spinning turns. The women's rage and terror keeps them howling and it becomes almost a chanting, singsong sound. It's a song of mourning and dread and its reverberated echo bouncing through the buried parking garage would spook and terrify us, if it weren't the only thing guiding us out. At each passageway the returning sound has a different texture, either an openness or a hollowed endlessness. It's obvious which way to turn.

We swerve and skid and barrel through the skinny passages, swirling up the twisting spirals. There's no easing up or backing off, I know the danger of confinement and constriction and suffocation. There's nothing more deadly. The helplessness, the unrighteousness, from a mute dumb victim's point of view. A passenger in the wrong plane, or ship, or body. I can't stand it. I have to be the one steering. Even so, who's really driving? How can you be sure? Suddenly we burst up, and out. We speed down the curving causeway, feeding us back onto the surface streets. Anything's better than that suffocating tomb—even surface streets.

We stop at a red light and the solid wall of cross-traffic clogs the intersection ahead. The dead concrete air of the parking basement lies stagnant in my chest and I hang my head out the window, sucking in the night air. The light changes green without me noticing and the city bus beside us roars off, pumping black diesel exhaust in my open window and deep into my lungs. I choke and cough, nearly gagging. The cars behind and all around are honking. The women yell directions. It's a confusion of foreign languages and meaningless noise. I punch it, still gasping for air. We swerve through the traffic. Who knows where? I barely care.

The women are talking. One says something about a Type A personality. About somebody being stressed out. One leans forward from behind, her arms resting on my shoulders. She murmurs in my ear, Do you want to fuck us? With her palms she rubs my shoulders and chest, and starts working down. I can feel the suction, the pull of the vacuum in her. Whores are hollow, they're weak and needful of something. Their souls are partially hollowed out and that's what's tugging on you, they need to fill up that void. Everybody does—me too. It wants to be brim-full. If you had two souls they'd suck one right out of you. I can't take any chances, I have to stay clear.

Have to keep my distance. I shrug and push her hands away. "Not here," I say. "Not now." They know a place. Maybe they know a time. They give directions. I'm not listening. I drive. It's cold in the car. The whores have the sleeping bag. Again I think about the heater. We hadn't wanted to clutter things up. Besides, it's not supposed to be cold here.

Along one side of the road stretches a strip of park. Hobos wander through the straight boles of tall palms or lie bundled and sleeping on the grass. It's like after a battle, where the dazed survivors wander and the dead randomly lie. We stop at a red light as the left-turning traffic streams onto the boulevard from a street butting in. I glance to the side. A ragged man sprawls sitting against a lamppost. His legs lie straight out before him, making a V. His head flops slightly back, his mouth fringed with gray half-beard hangs partly open and his eyes are closed. His ripped overcoat hangs unbuttoned and his dirty white dress shirt is ripped open down the front, baring his chest. A man and a woman crouch half-lying beside him, nursing on his wasted breasts.

Something catches in my throat and I cough and gasp, sucking for air. I swerve to the shoulder and jam us in nose-first against the curb. You don't do a slick parking job with no reverse gear. I climb out and walk across the street, leaving the door hanging open. The pavement is tilted a little and I walk part-sidelong, crabbing to follow straight toward where I'm looking. I barely hear the women calling from the car, and the traffic braking and swerving and honking as cars speed around me. I'm staring at the gray man leaning against the lamppost. I stop a dozen yards away. A searing pain shoots up into my throat from deep down inside my chest. The man glances toward me with his eyes glazed over.

"It's happened," he murmurs.

"What's happened?" I say. The ragged man and woman keep licking and nibbling at his chest and nipples, not heeding me. They're ravenous.

"The virgin birth," he whispers. "It's a miracle."

I come closer to hear better. The edges of my vision are going fuzzy.

"See?" he says. "Twins. Jesus and Helen."

Something else draws me closer too. The burning sensation drops down into my belly. Suddenly I feel hungry. Then the stench of the three washes over me and I choke, gasping to breathe. I stagger into the park, away from the street, out of the light. My throat feels strangled and aching and I can't suck any air past into my scorched chest. In the dark under the trees I trip over something or somebody. It groans and I crawl through soggy grass into thick brush. I collapse and roll over onto my back, straining to breathe, forcing the air in and out. Something is screaming. Someone, somewhere. I try to block it out, I block everything out. Concentrate: in, out, in, out. Finally my breathing slows and quiets. I can hear the wind tossing the brush and the tree branches above. I open my eyes. The tree trunks groan and creak and the black limbs and fronds wave and jerk in the rising wind. They're silhouetted against a light gray sky. The low overcast is lit from below by the bright lights of the city, but down in the shadows it's black-dark. I feel rain on my face. I stand up. Something's bothering me. I've forgotten something. Maybe it's something I never yet knew. That's even worse.

The rain crashes down. I never knew it rained in Los Angeles. Not like this. I'm soaked and shivering. This is an Olympic Peninsula Rainforest rain. A rain you get on the westside in the lowland river valleys for forty days straight in October and November. It's a chilling rain. It pours down. It's only interrupted by the gusts of whining wind that scatter the rain and blow it sideways. I wade through the soaked brush in blind blackness. Then the ground gives way and I tumble and roll and sprawl in the watery mud below a broken clay cliff. I get up instantly and stride down the gravelly mud slope without checking whether I'm OK. I guess I am.

Tall thorny bushes block the way. I lean into them and keep slogging down. Suddenly I burst out of the tangled brush onto wet pavement. I wander a couple of lanes out, amazed by the lines of raised glistening white dots glued to the blacktop. They look way different up close, when you're not streaking past at 60 or 70. From the left comes a blur of lights, and a swerving and a honk and a crash behind me. The crashing goes on and on. I climb a low divider and keep going, running and stumbling across clear lanes of pavement to a low wire fence. I claw my way over and run shuffling across the wet broken sand. The waves boom and thud ahead. On the left grows a close-standing forest of black tarred pilings. A stairway leads up. I climb it.

The stands and stores and restaurants on the wharf stand closed and boarded-up and deserted. A few lights glow dimly from high up on posts. The wind and rain wash over my face and I walk toward it, out over the broken sea. I hear the ocean churning among the black pilings not far below the heavy planks. The watery wind gusts and drives me back a little, and to the side. I'm under a roof. It's dry. I fall over a low metal railing, thigh-high. Slowly my eyes begin to see. I lie among a cluster of bumper-cars. I climb into one and sit curled and snug, sideways with my knees pulled up and my arms folded in tight. The wind whistles around the car and the shivering dies away and the chill dissolves into a damp warmth.

I dream. I don't know whether I'm asleep. I dream most of the time whether I sleep or not and I've gradually lost the knack of knowing for sure when I'm asleep or awake. At first I was afraid that meant I'd lost the knack for knowing how to sleep. It's an art really, to know how to sleep and how to tell the difference. Like everything else, people who have it take it for granted. Now I'm really freaked out that it might mean I've lost the ability to wake up. Whatever it is I'm dreaming, I can't remember even as I'm dreaming it. It goes that fast. Now there's one more thing I've forgotten. That really bugs me, every time. It chaps my ass. If I could only convince myself that there's no need to try to keep track of all the things you keep forgetting. But it still bothers me, living my life knowing I've forgotten something vital.

Once I woke up and thought, Oh hell, I had a whole life and for years now I've entirely forgotten it. What I think is my memory is probably entirely made up. Do any of these people and places really happen? Maybe I made it all up to help protect me from another memory—and it worked so well that I forgot for years and years that I once had a job and a wife and kids and a mortgage and an entire life and I just completely forgot about it all, by mistake. There was never any deceitful intent or anything. It just slipped my mind one day and I started living a different life and they're still back there in Cleveland or Kansas City, living day to day.

For the thousandth time I take long hard stock and try to think, did I? *Did I?* Something got lost all right. I'm just not sure what it was. Or who.

I'm stiff and aching in the tiny car and I get out and stretch. I'm not soaked any more, only damp. The gray is still dark, but lighter than before. The rain is a misty sprinkling that my skin barely feels when I walk out into it. The sea is gray and lumpy with white tumbling crests, louder now in the absence of wind. The tide is high and the waves spout up through the narrow cracks in the massive planking as the waves roll in. You can watch the spurting advance come down the pier and time your jump to try to stay dry. If it matters. I face the other way, toward the land.

A black limousine stands gleaming dully in the graying dark. It's parked near the foot of the ramp that leads up toward the city streets. The car is covered with glistening wet and the windshield wipers sweep slowly, with long pauses. Only the amber parking lights shine.

I approach from the passenger side. As I come closer I see inside, lit dimly by a low lamp in the car. Through a round window like a ship's porthole I see her lovely face. I never imagined what it would be like to see her again. I want to fall to my knees and crawl to her, weeping. I want to shout to her, and grin, and beckon her from the car. I do nothing. I come nearer, staring at her profile. Her face begins to turn toward me. Then the headlights come on and the car wheels to the right. The glaring white light blinds me and I shield my face with my arms. They pull past and curve away, humming up the ramp and over and out of sight. I stand on the abandoned pier in the drizzle and watch.

The rear license plate is the last thing I see. It lies burning in my brain. "DRS WIFE." How could you ever forget something like that? But I've forgotten all kinds of unimaginable things. I have to write it down. There's nothing to write with, or on. I roll up my sleeve and pull a rusted staple from a creosote lamppost. A scrap of a tattered handbill comes with it. I read, in bold black letters, "MAN IN A CAGE." Below that starts a quote, "After 35 years…" Jesus! Do I still have nine years to go? And then what? The sodden scrap of paper dissolves between my fingers. I notice the rusty staple pinched between my thumb and forefinger. Now, what? The license plate! It's almost gone, that quick. Things happen fast in Los Angeles. I recall it: "DRS WIFE." I use the staple to scratch the letters in my arm. I don't take any chances. I scratch deep, in the soft white inside of my forearm where no hair grows and the blue veins glow through the skin.

I roll my sleeve down over the bleeding wound and walk up the arching overpass. It's lighter now but the hump in the ramp blocks my view of what lies ahead. I rise with the concrete, and a great bustling slowly spreads out before me. I stand on the street corner with the traffic speeding past both ways. The pavement is already drying.

Somebody comes up behind me from under the overpass to the pier. I spin around. It's a man draped in kelp. The long slimy whips hang in large loose loops around his neck and shoulders. The tangled brown ribbons growing from the bulbs of the kelp flutter down from his shoulders like overgrown epaulettes. He stares straight at my eyes. It's a long stare. I see terror in his eyes. Maybe not. I see something. He probably doesn't know what it is either. He isn't sure he has it quite right. That's how it looks to me. That is, he believes he's the only one who isn't sure he has it right. He doesn't realize that everyone's like that. There are all those times when you suddenly feel a sinking dread, that you have it all wrong and everyone's laughing behind your back. You keep turning around fast, trying to catch them with their hands over their mouths, watching you with their laughing glancing eyes. Only you never quite catch them.

He's still staring at me. As if, well, people drape themselves and go marching off each morning, right? Don't they? *Don't they?* So, am I doing it right?

I think so. I like his style. I smile. He lurches back a little, his eyes going wider. Now he's more scared. I glance away but he still stares at me. His air washes over me and the smell is cold and briny and a little rotten.

The traffic is stopped for the light and I start across the street. His aroma follows me and I can still smell him. Maybe he's a god that came up out of the sea and thinks nobody can see him. Maybe nobody can. Why was I the only one? Maybe the deserted pier is his domain and he's haunting me for trespassing. By the time I reach the far sidewalk I can't smell him any more. I look back. He's not there. That is, I can't see him. At least he's not haunting me.

I keep going. I pass a newspaper vending machine and a bold black headline snags my eye. "POLICE CHIEF SAYS FREEWAY SHOOTINGS NOT A NEW THING." Oh, that's good. Wait a second. Something about it seems personal, somehow. What could anything in a headline have to do with me? I stand still on the sidewalk, staring into space, trying to think. I'm staring at a billboard. A huge pack of cigarettes is painted on it. In thick black letters the words, "ONLY ONE MILLIGRAM." It amazes me, that they come right out and tell you. Smoke one of these, pal, and you're going to get a milligram of tar in your lungs. Wow. Tar. My arm itches and I scratch it. That brings a stinging pain. I remember the words etched there. Here's a phone booth. Nobody swiped the phone book yet. I look on the page for state offices and find DMV. Colorado Street. I glance at the street sign on the corner. Colorado.

I keep walking. Seventeen blocks from the pier stands a hideous low green building. They must have been cheap to build this way in the fifties. All the recent government buildings when I was a kid looked like this. If you keep your credit cards loaded up, you have two good reasons not to feel so bad if the ozone layer dissolves completely and all life on the planet dies out.

Inside I stand in a long line. I shuffle with the rest. Finally I stand at the endless counter. A woman sits on the other side. She glances up through her glasses.

"Yes?"

"I want to find out about a license plate."

"What kind of license plate?"

"Where people write what they want, in seven letters or less," I say.

"Personalized plate. They're twenty-five dollars a year. Did you check the book?"

"What book?"

"There." She points. "The catalogue of all the personalized plates. Go ahead," she says, "see if you find it in the book."

I go where she says and leaf through a thick tome. Thousands and thousands of words and mottos and slogans, most of them stupid. Alphabetized. "DRS WIFE" is missing. I wait in line again, shuffling with the others.

"It's not there," I say.

"You're in luck then," she says.

"In luck?"

"If it's not in the book then it's still available. Do you want to submit an application?"

"I want to find out who has it."

"Nobody has it, if it's not in the book."

"But I just saw it on a car."

"Not if it's not in that book," she says. "Unless it's a recent issue. Are you sure it was a California plate?"

"Yes."

"What was it? I'll check the computer for you."

I pull back my sleeve, wincing a little when the fabric drags across the scar. The letters are raised and swollen and trickle blood.

"Huh," she says. "I'd be very surprised if that wasn't already...let's see." She rattles away on the computer, waits watching the screen, and frowns. "Nope. No such plate. That's really amazing." She glances up and shrugs. "Sorry. Unless, of course, you want the plate yourself."

"No, thank you." I want something else. I don't know what. I walk outside. Something is wrong. More wrong than I knew before. The sun is out and the pale glare blinds me. I'm freezing. No warmth from that sun. Why? It's supposed to be hot here. I always heard it was. How can a palm tree live in this climate? You need sunglasses and a down parka. Glacier goggles and an insulated spacesuit. The glare is killing me. The white cement sidewalks shoot searing white waves straight through my eyes into my brain. And the cold! The landscape is as bright and harsh and frozen as the moon. It has the white colorlessness of horseradish. I squint my eyes nearly shut and reel down the hard sidewalk, snowblind. The numbness is oozing inward from my toes and fingertips, creeping up my shins and forearms.

I crash into a loaded shopping cart and stumble to my hands and knees on the sidewalk. The cart careens toward the curb and a crone screams and runs after it. I open my eyes wide, braving the burning pain. My throat is tight and burning too, making it hard to take more than shallow panting breaths. I try to swallow and it feels like someone has grated on my throat with a steel rasp. I look up, remembering about smog. But the sky is blue straight up. I look all around—we're surrounded by a thick brownish yellow haze. The smog is all around, only we are spared. But it doesn't feel that way. I can feel it grating my throat with every breath. This is the thing about smog: you can't see it looking straight up. It's invisible from close-up. You can only see it from a distance, or looking edge-on. You don't know what trouble you're in once you're in it, only before, or after you get out and happen to glance back. It's like truth, or like the galaxy, which looks brighter from a distance when all the stars blend together in a murky glow.

A wheel of one of the loaded shopping carts rolls over the fingers of my left hand—I'm sitting on the sidewalk staring at the sky. The pain in my fingers gets me to my feet. The crone is hustling around trying to corral her three shopping carts. They're crammed with mounds of treasures and arti-facts, all bagged neatly in tattered white plastic Vons bags. She keeps getting two of the carts under control and then the third goes rolling slowly off down the gentle grade toward the sea, seventeen blocks away. I don't know how she was managing before I came barging in and knocked her off kilter.

Finally two carts get loose at once and at the last moment I rescue one from tottering off the sidewalk into the street. I turn to her, offering her the cart. She grips her other two with white knuckles and stares at me—I stagger three steps back, clutching the cart to keep from falling. I stare at her eyes, stunned and mesmerized—she has kelpman eyes. She looks way older than he but people aren't always how they look. Her face is pure white except for her cheeks, which are covered with huge purplish-red circles of rouge. Her hair is white and thin and straggling down. She wears brand-new black hightop Converse basketball shoes, without socks, and the ragged remains of something skirt-like. Above that is something that resembles a sleeveless sweater or sweatshirt, the faded gray color of street-dust. It bulges out in front, rounded and swelling like a huge paunch, only lumpy and uneven rather than smooth. At first you think she's as fat as Santa Claus. Then you see she has the sweater stuffed with hundreds of flattened aluminum cans. Maybe a thousand. Maybe more.

And she's looking at me that same way: Do I have it right? She doesn't know either, that she isn't the only one who suspects she doesn't. Isn't this how they do it? They stash their wealth and their valuables close to their chest, I've seen them. Don't they? *Don't they!* What is it, oh God what in the world is it? What's wrong? Why don't they say yes, why don't they smile and clasp my hand, embrace, make those meaningless sounds that I would make back, if only I knew if only! Why those looks, those glances—averted glances, terrified glances. Please can't you see, *I'm* the one who's scared. Too scared to talk. Too scared to make a peep. Too scared to loosen the grip on my cart, too scared to sleep because someone could make off with my cans, my treasure, my wealth. Can't you see how I'm trying? Can't anyone see?

Her stare goes to the cart I'm holding. Then back to my face. I smile. Her eyes widen, more scared than before.

"There's someone you should meet," I say. She doesn't say anything. "Down this way." I nod toward the beach. "Come on." I start out, slow, pushing the one cart and smiling over my shoulder at her. She comes along behind, pushing the other two, watching me.

"Want some help?" I say. "I think I can handle two. Be like a holiday for you, just handling the one." I stop and reach for her near cart. But she draws back, sucking her breath in and clenching her teeth.

"All right, it's OK. Just wanted to help. Not horning in or

nothing, don't want any of your loot, not that it's not great stuff and all but, hey, I travel light, you know?"

Another ten feet and I start appreciating her judgment in not letting me take on a second cart. I happen to be lucky enough to have the one with the busted wheel. No wonder she lives on the fringe. There's nothing more challenging than manhandling a loaded shopping cart with one sprung wheel. There are plenty of CEOs making the big bucks who wouldn't be able to handle it. I begin to appreciate her ability to even survive—the cart heads off in every direction but where I want it to go. It's a nightmare. There's no way we're covering seventeen blocks. The question is whether I'll get it as far as the gas station half a block away.

I hear a musical sound and look over. The Baglady in Rouge is laughing. She has a new face, she has become lovely. She glances away, too polite to let on she's laughing at me.

Finally we reach the gas station. I'm drained. Maybe I can park her somewhere and bring the kelpman to her. It's doubtful he can survive this far from the water, but what are the options? Something flickers, maybe it's my eye twitching. Something seems to glow or rhythmically pulsate at the edge of my sight, half-behind me. I turn to look. A long van without side windows is parked at the pumps. It's a late model but it has no paint job at all. Or rather, a paint job the exact color of rust. I wheel over, leaning on the cart like one of those three-wheeled walkers. On the way I check out the license plate. It's a hideous obsession, reading license plates. I can't pass without looking. In this case: DP42867. Christ! Forty-two thousand disabled persons in the state. Or, who knows how many more? I touch the paint job, only it isn't paint. Rust, after all. It's a beautiful rust, blended of light and dark swirls and blotches and mottles.

Someone up toward the front of the van is yelling. I look around the corner. The gas station man, blond-headed, is yelling in some brutal accent that massacres the language. Maybe it's an American accent, maybe not. I don't recognize it. I don't care.

"Self-service only!" he shouts. "Nothing wrong with you, get out of the car and pump your own gas." He turns away, back toward the office.

"Excuse me," I call. "I'll pump the gas." I move forward along the side of the van and he comes back, looking me up and down.

"Pay first," he says.

A slender hand with finely etched tattoos across the back and lacing the fingers reaches from the driver's window, holding cash. I walk past and brush her hand back inside. I stand before the blond man. He's my age, maybe older, maybe not. He's my height.

"Pay in advance," he says.

I say, "Turn on the pump or I'll kill you."

He stares at me. "What?" he says finally.

"This is America. Turn on the pump."

He does. Then he hurries to the office and disappears. I fill the tank. Part of a young woman's face watches me in the big side mirror as I work the nozzle. The face is clear of all expression. What I can see of it. Wide eyes, smooth white skin, pale lips. The hollow curve of her cheek.

I screw the cap on tight and the van's rear door swings open.

"Hey we could use a lift," I call to her. "Do you mind?" She watches in the mirror and doesn't speak. I nod to the woman in rouge and we push the carts to the rear of the van and she helps me lift them in. You'd be surprised at her strength. I am.

63

I glance forward. Between the two front seats is propped a folded wheelchair. She watches us in the mirror. From behind I see she has three shades of hair, violet and black and rose, left to right. We get the carts in and the rougelady scrambles in between them. I walk around to the passenger door, trailing my hand along the side of the van. My palm comes away rust-brown. I like it that color.

The door is unlocked and I climb in and sit down. We pull out of the gas station. I settle into the soft seat, it fits me. I feel rested suddenly. A relaxation comes over me and I sigh, breathing slow and easy. I look over. She sits nestled in the chair, her thin legs canted to one side. She wears sweatpants, thin white socks and scuffed red and green suede bowling shoes. Her blouse is antique lace and for a necklace she wears a string of black-tarnished silver baby spoons.

She glances over. Not a detail of her face changes. It's a porcelain deathmask.

"We're headed for the beach," I say. "You mind?"

She turns left and drives us to the top of the ramp leading down to the pier. We wait at the left-turn light.

"We're looking for someone," I say. "A man dressed in kelp. I last saw him right around here."

We turn left and drive slowly down the curb lane. Three guys stand around in front of a liquor store. I roll down the window and she slows to a stop, double-parked. I call out to them, asking if they've seen a man dressed in kelp. They don't speak English, shake their heads, jabbering. The next four people we ask don't speak English either. Then an old ragged man who doesn't speak at all. He stands staring at me, drooling into his beard. We turn off the main street and slowly follow a maze of winding lanes and alleys through crowded old beach cabins and two- and three-story crumbling apartments piled all on top of each other. We ask more people about the man in kelp and finally someone points, That way, farther down.

The twisting road grazes the sand at the beach. I ask her to stop, and step out for a look at open sky and a far-off rolling horizon that isn't man-made. But that's impossible here. A city of cardboard shacks and visqueen and canvas tents stretches for hundreds of yards across the sand. The tilted and half-limp tent-peaks jaggedly break the skyline. The kelpman could live here. I wander among the tents, finding people in pairs and clusters and alone, talking, sleeping, singing. Some are ragged, some not. Some are old, some are foreigners, some are drooling on themselves. Some are just about everything. Maybe they all came to L.A. to be heroes. Maybe they are. Maybe not; maybe they're thinking about something else. Maybe they aren't the least functional level of the would-bees and the wannabees and the can't-bees. Maybe they're not the bottom layer in the star parfait. Maybe they checked out of that hotel. Maybe some of them see any hotel as just one more robber of attention. Maybe not.

Most of them know of the kelpman. They point every different direction, up the beach, down the beach, inland, out to sea.

From the north end of the tent city comes the guttural roar of diesel engines. Three big D-9 Cats are grinding south, uprooting the tents and shacks and lean-tos with their wide bulldozer blades. Black soot spouts from their flappered stovepipe exhausts. People scream and scramble from the collapsing huts and run all different ways. A young woman, maybe she's still a teenager, staggers by holding a baby and pulling a toddler along by the hand. She's sobbing. Behind the bulldozers comes a line of cops in gas masks and riot helmets, wielding clubs. A tear gas canister comes lobbing over the machines and lands a few yards downwind of me, billowing smoke. I take a breath and squeeze my eyes shut tight and grope for the canister—I find a grip, heft it and heave it back. I open my eyes and see it flying over the cats and past the cops, soaring like a glider. Someone shouts close to my ear and I turn and run.

I make it back to the van and we drive on. We keep asking. Several people have seen the kelpman. We pull into a big open parking lot fronting the ocean sand. A skinny concrete pier juts out, a long narrow walkway on a single row of concrete pilings leading to a square blockhouse. All along the pier people are fishing. Their poles stick out down the whole length of the pier like thin spines on a giant sea creature.

I get out of the van. From the back comes a crash and clatter. The rougelady has unloaded the carts herself. I help her right them and heap the treasures back in. We ask a woman with a fishing pole about the kelpman. She points out to sea. We walk to the edge of the pavement, as far as the carts can go, and scan the ocean. It's covered with floating litter and trash. I always wondered what happened in a land without rain, to the dog shit and cat piss and cigarette butts and styrofoam coffee cups. Now I know. A couple times a year it all washes into the sea. Better not go swimming for a week or two after a rain.

Now I make him out, bobbing in the water underneath the pier. I shout and point. Nobody hears. The driver is still in the van and the lady in rouge is down along the surfline, picking through the washed-up litter.

He swims shoreward, heavily loaded. It's slow going, weaving through curtains of fishing lines. Maybe it's him they're trying to catch. It's magical how he weaves through the tangle of lines and never snags his long trailing train of fresh kelp. On he comes, boosted by the surge of the swell. A breaking wave catches him and he skims in, riding it out and finally standing up in knee-deep foam. He's wrapped and draped in the glossy brown kelp and he strides ashore clothed in it, with long supple strands streaming off in cryptic and far-reaching patterns and designs.

He comes ashore near the lady in rouge. She's bent over sorting among found treasures when she first sees him—she freezes, staring at him, and slowly stands up straight. He sees her, and contemplates her for long moments. Gradually he moves across the foamy sand and stops before her. The draping curtains of kelp hide his legs and he seems to float. Maybe he is floating. Without taking his eyes from her face he disentangles a long supple kelp whip, and offers it to her. Her mouth falls open, she gawks at the beauty of it. Clumsily she fumbles in her baggy pouched sweatshirt for a handful of flattened cans and holds them out to him. But he shakes his head, smiling. She drops the cans in the sand as he reaches out, coiling the kelp like a tiara in her hair, and draping and looping the ends around her neck and shoulders.

I turn away. The van is gone. I walk across the wide empty parking lot, not looking back. It's slow going. Walking feels inefficient. It's a flat desert with a palm oasis here and there. Bicycles pass, racing against something. They almost cream me. It's up to me to get out of the way. They're more efficient.

Just outside the parking lot exit stands the rusted van, listing with one flattened tire. No wonder. She'd driven out across the angled teeth set in the pavement to keep you from driving out that way. I glance up and down the parking lot. All the entrances and exits have the teeth angled the same way, inside. Once you get in there's no getting out. No wonder the lot is empty. You need local knowledge to make it around here. Somehow she'd managed to rupture only one tire.

It's not my fault. I mean, *fault*. What the hell is that? People just do what they do. That's all. Then somebody does something else. Fault doesn't ever even enter into it. It's like guilt. There's no such thing. I don't believe in either of them. Belief is a matter of choice, right? They both have to do with control, laid on from outside. I don't believe in that either. That's not even a matter of choice. There's no such thing. Control comes from somewhere else. One place. Inside. If you don't know that you'll never learn the difference between right and wrong. Between weakness and strength. Between joy and sorrow. Freedom and slavery. Life and death.

I walk up to the driver's window. She sits still as ever, staring ahead.

"Where's the jack?"

She turns her head to stare at me. Then, almost imperceptibly, her eyes move toward the left. I go around to the back. The door is ajar. I get out the jack and spare and change the tire. I put the jack and the wrecked tire back in and walk away, across the street.

"Hey," I hear someone say. I turn around. The womb-man is staring at me. "Do you know where you're going." She says it in a flat voice, like a challenge.

I laugh. Then I cross the street and get in. We drive. She pulls into an alley and parks, opens her door, lifts the wheelchair over and snaps it open, sets it on the ground and lowers herself into it in a strong smooth motion.

Bordering the alley is a tall, sagging cyclone fence with

barbed wire on top, all intertwined and overgrown with a flowering bush. The blossoms hang in walls of scarlet and purple and pumpkin, and I want to go up close and bury my face in them and breathe deeply. Something makes me look closer first, I'm paranoid. I was lured and scarred by roses as a child. For once, I learned from the past—I remember and avoid costly lacerating repetitions of a basic lesson. The flowers aren't flowers at all, just colored leaves concealing long brown needle-spines. I sniff from a distance but there's no smell, except for the hint of an aroma from the womb-man. She smells of snow.

The imposter-flowers overarch a low narrow gateway she opens with a key. Inside we cross a muddy yard to an old stucco building with a slanting sheetmetal roof. Over the double doors is painted, in large faded lavender letters, "Powerhouse." She unlocks these and we go into a dimly lit high-ceilinged place, empty and open like an abandoned warehouse. Out on the floor, not in the center, stands a cage. Like a coffin standing on end, only slightly wider and not as tall. There's a man in the cage, lying on his back with his legs stretched out straight upward, resting against the bars. He's singing or chanting or muttering, softly, in a rhythmic way that echoes and reverberates with itself in the high empty building.

She wheels across the flagstone floor to the cage. I follow. He doesn't notice us. I can hear him better now. It sounds like English but I can't understand a word of it. The woman closely examines the cage. She touches and peers at the welds at the corners, and where the bars join. The man drones on. Somehow it's musical. It begins to mean something. Not that I understand any of the words, or sounds. His white hair and beard are long and wispy. He wears some kind of ripped cloak or cape, and lies on what's left of an old wool army blanket. I walk around to see his face better. His eyes are very young. He looks like a child in the body of an old man. He stares into space, at nothing. Or, who knows? Suddenly he's silent. In the eaves of the building the pigeons begin cooing. He answers them.

He moves suddenly, sliding in the cramped cage with amazing ease and grace into a sitting position. The way he moves is a dance.

"Where is she?" he says, not looking at me, not locking onto anything specific, with his eyes shifting around in space.

I look around the room. She's gone. Rain begins to fall on the metal roof.

"Aaah," he says, in a long sigh, glancing up. The skin on his face is dirty and scabbed and flaking. But you can see joy coming out right through the skin. Or wonder. Something. Something people would want for themselves if they knew about it.

"I've noticed she doesn't talk much," I say.

"She talks," he says. "Only she listens, too." His eyes are still moving, not attaching to anything. "She built the cage," he says. "It's a masterpiece," and his gaze focuses on a detail of the cage, and he touches and examines it, humming or purring to himself, or to someone, or something.

"Yeah," I say. "By the way, what are you doing in there?"

He glances sharply at me, grazing me with his eyes for the first time. He stares straight into my face. "What are you doing out there?" he says.

"What?"

"Never mind. I plagiarized that. Cauthorn says everything's plagiarized. Unless you make up your own language you're

70

just copying what you heard before and combining it a little differently. That's how Guthrie came up with his melodies. Ripped 'em off. Nobody makes up the idea of language. We all plagiarize that. Aesirssen made up his own language, he says, but it sounds a lot like English to me. He took the opposite tack and said that everyone makes up their own language and spews it out and sometimes we think someone else thinks they have some idea what we're trying to say. As if we have any idea ourselves. Or maybe it was I who said that. Anyway, I guess I just did. I think. Maybe. I think. Imagine that. The presuppositions! You could spend lifetimes exploring the uncorroborated hypotheses. Implicit. *Implicit.* Maybe I will. Maybe I have. Maybe I am. Maybe. Jesus, *maybe!*"

"Hey," I say, looking at the latch. "There's no lock, you can get out of there any time you want.

"Really." He says it somewhere between amazement and something else. There's so much in it he distracts himself. "Reeeaaaally," he says.

"Hey why don't you come out?"

"Why don't you come in?"

"Uh, no thanks," I say, feeling a tightening in my throat.

"You seem to have a stake in getting me to come out."

"Well, sure. There's a lot going on out here."

"Reeeeeaaaaaaaally," he says, twisting in on the word.

"There's lots to do."

"Too much to do to come out, that's for sure."

The restriction in my throat is growing, cinching down on the air passage. That stifled feeling is growing in my chest. The slow burn that never quite stops smoldering. "What's going on here, anyway," I say.

For a while he can't talk. He's choking for air too, only his is from laughing, silently. Finally he gasps out, "What's going on here, anyway. See, that's what I'm trying to find out. I think. I thinkkk."

I don't hear the rest. I have to get out before my throat clamps down the rest of the way and I collapse on the flagstones. I stumble outside, blinded in the pale white light, my eyeballs seared. I trip over something. I'm on my hands and knees in gravelly sand staring at a tarnished DeSoto hood ornament. But only for a moment—suddenly I'm struck between the eyes with a visceral force that reverberates through my skull and frame and knocks me to my feet and several steps backward, staggered and reeling.

"Jesus Christ my car!" I yell out loud, as memory washes back over me in ringing waves of recollection. "My God!" And I run out through the gate to the alley. The van is parked there. She's sitting in the driver's seat, staring dead ahead.

"Quick, get going, hurry, please!" I yell, hurrying around and jumping into the passenger seat. Slowly she turns to look at me. There's the trace of an expression on her face, surprise, irritation, I don't know. "Come on," I shout. "It's an emergency, my car, oh God my car, I can't believe it! Please, can't you get moving?"

She stares at me, not moving.

"Start the damned truck!" I yell.

"You have a car?" she says, with her face, unused to asking a question, in an odd cast.

"Do I have a car? Yes, somewhere. I had a car. Come on, we got to—Christ, what a car! The pier, when we first hit the beach, remember? Yeah. Jesus what a car. It goes over 200 miles an hour, on the freeway, from Ephrata to Moses Lake Atticus and I—would you please start the damned van!"

Something flickers across her face. Surprise, maybe. Curiosity. Desire? How should I know? I see it. You don't always understand what you see. When you think you do you're so often wrong. And if you're not, there isn't always a name for it. She starts the van and drives us along unknown streets. My mind feels numb. I can hardly think. How long? We left it sitting there, with the door hanging open. Skewed nose-first into the curb with the ass end sticking out in the bike lane. Did I even turn off the engine? There's no key, would the whores figure out how to work the switch under the dash?

It doesn't make sense. Not a trace of logic or necessity or reason. What could have—how the hell could I forget about my car? Sure, I live with vast gaping gaps in my memory— doesn't everyone? Sometimes I have no idea what's happened and what hasn't. Maybe most of the time. That could be why I'm telling all this, just trying to keep track. But to lose track of the *car?* It's insane. All that about clarity, purity, essence, all that bullshit—did I just forget? All the single-minded purposefulness and obsession—I came here on a mission! Who—what—where was I? What the hell happened? Is this what L.A. does to you? Is this how it all came about, why these people live this way, the freeway crawl, the brain-death, the spirit-cancer, the laugh-pinch, the breath-choke-gasp? The first impression so horrifying and hypnotizing and brain-boggling that we lose all sense of why we came in the first place, and never get back even the merest shred of a memory of why we're here?

If it weren't for the car, maybe I'd be lost forever too. That's my salvation, that my dream has a concrete form. Or rather, a concrete accessory. Otherwise I'd be just another zombie, with evaporated dreams that never left even a residue of their passing. That's the standard routine. I'm lucky to be alive.

My breathing settles down, deeper, more rhythmic. My pulse is still hammering through every pipeline in my body.

The cars and streets and businesses and stoplights blur past.

"I've got to get out," I say. "Get my car and get the hell out."

She speaks without taking her eyes off the road. "That's right. Get out while you can." She pulls to a stop. The road is barricaded. Beyond the wooden barricades stands a solid wall of people, all with their backs to us.

"What is this?" I say, and get out of the van. What can it mean? Does everything that happens, every circumstance, mean more than itself, or less than itself, or anything at all? That's the entire question. Lots of wars are fought over it. Philosophy is the basis of all conflict and warfare. Bad philosophy that is. Sloppy thinking. Irrationality. Illogic. It's an attitude. You nip it in the bud, or it nips you—and you die in a stranger's yard, a corollary to some megalomaniac's tirade. Don't do it. I won't if you won't. No, I take that back. I won't whether you do or not.

The nasal drone of Scottish bagpipes drifts over the crowd. I crane to see through the people. A highlander marching band is sweeping past in green plaid kilts, blaring out their weird buzzing music that betrays all their pretenses and illusions of being actually civilized. I stare at them, awed and amazed. Bagpipes! I want to wear a kilt and blow on the pipes and march with them. Always wanted to. But the car—what the hell's the matter with me? Don't get distracted by a bunch of bagpipes. Get going. Keep going. Get the hell out. I go back to the van.

"It's a parade," I say. "We got to find a detour. How far to the pier?"

"Across the street," she says, still staring ahead.

"Oh, no. That means—I'm parked on the parade street, it might be hours before I can get my car out." She turns and gazes at me with a new look I haven't seen, and the realization hits me and I run out and push through the crowd to check. Hell! All the cars are gone. A row of pedestrian cops lines the street, controlling the crowd. I run up to the nearest one.

"My car," I yell over the drone of the bagpipes. "Where the hell's my car?"

"Excuse me, sir?"

"My car, it was parked right there."

He glances over his shoulder at the crowd-lined curb. "Temporary tow-away zone, sir. Check the OPG."

"What the hell's the OPG?"

He gazes at me for a moment before answering. He's my age or younger, hoping to come off a certain way. "Official Police Garage," he says.

I reel back to the van and stand outside the open passenger door. "I'm fucked. Christ I don't believe it—I'm an idiot!"

"What happened?" she says.

"They towed it. God, of all the luck, a damned parade—how could I do that? I just...walked off. Left it there with the door open and the engine running, for all I know. All 'cause I saw some old kook sitting on the sidewalk with a man and lady hobo nursing on his breasts."

"What?"

"Yeah. I mean, so what? You see nuts every day doing amazing things. It's not exactly worth losing your car over." I got in the van and slammed the door. "Shit!"

"Do you have the money to get it out?"

"Money? That's got nothing to do with it. There's a standing warrant out for my arrest. I got no I.D. There's no registration, no serial numbers, no valid license plate, no blinkers. There's no make or model or year, I got no way of identifying the car to them. There's no reverse gear!"

"What kind of car is it?"

"It's a one-off, I built it myself—well, Atticus and I."

"You built your own car?"

Her voice catches my attention. I look at her. She's contemplating me with a new strange look. Suspicious, maybe. Maybe something else.

"Yeah," I say. "I told you, it goes over 200 miles an hour. That's why I came here."

"A one-of-a-kind car like that, should be easy to track it down. What color is it?"

"Well, yeah. See, that's another problem. It was blue, I think. No, red."

"You think. You don't know what color it was?"

"Sure, red," I say. "But under that it's white, then blue, then red, and so on, like that. See the body's made of wood. Cedar, cold-molded, it's varnished bright as a mirror. There's an inlay—at least Atticus had plans for one. I never got a look at it, he worked all night and he was already laying on the adhesive sheets when I got there. Camouflage. We peel off a layer each time we make a speed run. Takes a few seconds. Sometimes we go so fast the wind peels off a layer or two on its own. You'll see, I'll show you. If I ever get the car back. Christ, the Official Police Garage. What kind of SS outfit do you suppose that is?"

We sit in the van, silent. Plans and ideas ricochet around in my head. Some of them have nothing to do with the car or getting it back. Damn, at a time like now—at least *try* to concentrate. Fool! Maybe if that damned marching band would shut up. Will America never get tired of Sousa and his imposter-America? It's the opposite of what Clemens says about Wagner—Sousa is worse than it sounds.

"Maybe I can help," she says, and starts the van and backs up, turning around.

"Help what?"

"What do you think? Get your car back."

"Oh, yeah. I don't know what it is, something's wrong. I can't keep my mind on anything. I used to live like a damned torpedo. My brain worked like a missile. It homed in, you know? But now, it's buckshot. I used to punch big gaping holes and now I ricochet and scatter and fly off in every damned direction. Ever since I got to L.A.—no, it started before that. I don't even know when. I thought I knew why I came here. It was like I had a mission. Only, there's something inside me, wanting to bust out. Pulling me this way, and that. Half the time I can't breathe, my throat cinches down, my head throbs like I'm wearing a steel spring for a headband, torqued down to about half the diameter. I got this burning in my chest, it never goes away. Like it's too crowded in here, inside me. Like there's more than one of us in here, clamoring to have input. What's this all about? I never even heard of such a thing. Have you?"

"How long since you reached L.A.?"

"I don't know. I can't even remember. Let's see. Christ, it was yesterday. Last night. Rush-hour."

"It's always rush-hour here."

"Yeah, well, I just don't know. A week ago I never would've said that. 'I just don't know.' Bullshit. I've known for years, I can't remember when I didn't know. Only now..."

"L.A. does that to people," she says.

"I don't know, I think I—see, there it is again. Maybe it started before that. My sense of rhythm, my sense of pace, my control, I was losing that. I was getting rushed, and slowed. I always figured, how you feel depends on what you

77

think about. So you got to be careful what you think about. You got to be in control."

"Nobody's in control."

"Bullshit, I was in control. When you're flying across the Palouse at 200-plus, you're in control. You got to be right, that's all. It can be done—you just always have to be right."

"Who's always right?"

"You *have* to be. There's no other excuse for being alive. It's like, with Eskimos, you know? It's black and white."

"Eskimos."

"Yeah. There's no such thing as a neurotic Eskimo. Don't you see why? It's elemental. You eat or you die. You keep warm or you die. You win or you die. They're the original Americans, the very first. Every day they stay alive, they're the ultimate winners. If you're an Eskimo, you only have to lose once. Fall through the ice. Get munched by a polar bear. Then you're dead. It's that simple. Only, can't you see? It's the same for us. Exactly the same. Just slightly more subtle. Death comes slowly in L.A. It creeps up gradually. Look around. These people, they've all got slow-AIDS. They're still walking, but they're already dead. It's murder by suicide. Personally, I'd rather get it all at once from a polar bear. One big swat of his paw. One crunch of his nine-inch fangs. But then, I'm an American. Maybe one of the last. Or hopefully"—I glance at her and grin—"one of the first. You know?"

We stop at a stoplight. She drops her head down onto the steering wheel, and whispers, "I used to believe that."

"Yeah? Like, I couldn't wait at a light when nobody was coming. Wasn't right."

She glances up at me, then at the light. It stays red. We wait.

"Face it, we're all blowing this pop stand. The only question is, what you going to do in the meantime? You get good at what you practice, so you got to be real careful what you do, because you're always practicing. You got to start off doing what you want to end up doing. Otherwise you get real good at what you start off doing and forget where it was you wanted to get to. You know what Atticus always said? 'Consequences are important only if you're a wimp.' That's how I lived. That's how we lived. No compromise, no regret."

"Before yesterday," she says.

"I don't know. I got this baggage, and I don't even know what it is or where it came from. Look, I'm just guessing here. I went to see my sister, and there was this baby waiting to be born. Trying to be born. It died and we buried it in the snow. I keep thinking about it. Not thinking about it, but working all the time not to think about it. I keep remembering what the dad wanted to name it, Crazy Horse. Someone says But Crazy Horse was a man, and he says, Well, whatever. I don't remember if this was before or after she died. Before, I guess. It's funny, see I always had this thing about Crazy Horse. Now there was an American."

A car honks behind us. I look up, the light's green. That was Crazy Horse's doing. I glance at the womb-man. She stares straight ahead with her pure blank face, and tears run down her porcelain cheeks.

"Better an untimely death..." she whispers, murmuring, and her lips barely move. I lose the rest of what she says.

"What?" I say quietly.

The cars behind start honking in chorus. She jerks, snapping her head up suddenly, and jams on the throttle with her right hand and we lurch ahead.

"If you want I can help," she says. "I can forge anything

you want. Registration, documents, citations."

"What, you're a forger?"

"I used to be an artist," she says.

"Used to be."

She gives me a level gaze. "Yes," she says.

"Bullshit."

Her face takes on a new look, maybe of puzzlement and pride, or hurt and surprise, an inkling of rage. She glances back to the road. I watch her face, in profile. The slick tear track still marks her cheeks, unwiped and unsmeared.

"You can't used to be an artist. There's no such thing. An artist always does art. Can't help it."

"Then why are you so hot to get your car back. It shouldn't make any difference."

"I never said there's no difference. Everything has its own magic, you know?"

"Fuck magic," she says.

"So you're not doing art anyone can see or hear or smell. Or buy. You're still doing it."

"If you're going to keep on with this shit, why don't you just get out of the fucking car," she says.

"Fine. Don't start telling me what I can talk about. Let me out here."

With her left hand she snags the brake, and swerves over to the curb. We both sit waiting. Slowly she glances at me, with something like a scowl. "Well?" she says.

I look out the window, at the writing on the stores. There's a huge hammer and sickle flag painted on the wall of a brick building, and the slogan, "Welcome to Soviet Monica." I look up at the sky. It's yellow.

I glance across at her. She's still scowling, straight ahead now. "I got to get my car back," I say. She looks at me, looking irritated. I grin. "Hey, you said you'd help me." I shrug. "I admit it, I need help. I mean, I can live without it. But it would, you know, help."

She peers down at her side mirror and pulls out into the traffic. We get on the freeway. It's packed. Lanes and lanes and lanes clogged with cars, mile after mile. We stop, we creep, and so on. Slow swerves around twisted bumpers and broken taillights and flattened chrome strips. Doesn't anybody ever pick any of this shit up? The air gets thicker and thicker. Every car has one person in it, the driver. We're freaks, with two in the van. But nobody notices, nobody stares. They're comatose.

Momentarily we get to use the diamond lane. Us, and the buses. It only takes two to make a carpool in L.A. We hum along at sixty down the one skinny vacant lane, beside the six-lane parking lot. Someone in the fast lane that isn't moving opens their window and chucks out a bag of trash right in front of us. We cream it and scatter flimsy cans and fastfood cartons all over the pavement. The concrete sections click past under the tires. It feels faster being up over the pavement with no hood out front. I long to settle down and stretch out in my sedan, lower her down mere inches off the pavement and wind her out. If the buses weren't so thick you could use the diamond lane to show these nerds. I'm so hungry for it my mouth waters. My sweaty palms itch and the sole of my right foot tingles, craving to be jammed down on something solid, like my gas pedal bottomed out on the sheetmetal floorboards. But with the buses you couldn't get much over 140 before having to stand on the brakes. Still, you can dream. We dream.

We're off the freeway. We drive through a flat country of abandoned warehouses and dead-end railroad tracks and broken concrete and industrial supplies. Signs are written in a foreign language. Spanish, I guess.

We park on the street and I follow her to a high blank-faced building. She rolls up a ramp to a loading dock. She won't let me push. We go in through a wide freight door of metal slats that rolls up clanking when she pushes a button. Inside is space and shadows. She rolls down the door behind us and the shadows take over. I stay still in the quiet dark. I hear her quiet rubber wheels rolling over the slick concrete floor. A spotlight flicks on. It's aimed straight up at the high ceiling and it lights the room in a gloom that deepens toward the vague distant walls. If there are walls. I can't see any. What's off there, in the vague shadowy distance? Could be anything. I forget to look. She sits before a rough wooden worktable. That's all I notice. Like I said, you only have so much attention. She has mine. She leans over the table, working on a sheet of clean white paper with a quill pen that she now and then dips in a small pot of black indelible India ink.

I look over her shoulder. Across the top of the paper she draws "Order to Remove Government Property" in bold black calligraphy that looks like government engraving from the turn of the century. Below she prints small typewriter letters that have a grainy xeroxed look.

"Why don't you find out where they took the car," she murmurs without looking up from her work.

"Sure," I say. "Got a phone?"

"Yeah."

She doesn't say where. I look around and spot one, a heavy old black dial unit standing alone on the smooth concrete floor. The round black cord snakes away into the shadows. I call directory assistance and a man answers. I ask for the number for the OPG.

"Which one, sir?"

"Uh, which one?"

There's a pause. "That's what I said, sir. You think there's one OPG for the entire fucking city? There's twenty million people out there stretching as far as the imagination can see."

"Yeah, right," I say. I tell him Santa Monica and he gives me a number. He thanks me for using AT&T, or GT&E, or some three-letter outfit. Everything comes in three letters around here.

"You get the number?" she says. I glance over. She's bent over the paper, still not looking up.

"Yes."

"Bring me the phone." I set it on the tabletop. She lifts the receiver and crimps it between her shoulder and her ear. "Dial," she says.

I dial the number. She keeps writing on the form. She's two-thirds of the way down the sheet. Now, on the lower left, she's drawing up an official government seal. On the right are titles and signatures.

"This is Lieutenant Hildebrand, U.S. Naval Intelligence," she says into the phone. "We believe you have one of our ROVs in your custody."

A pause.

"Remote Operated Vehicle. We lost track of the vehicle near the intersections of Ocean Boulevard and Colorado in Santa Monica. I'd like to verify that you do have such a vehicle in your custody, so that we can send a man down to pick it up without any further loss of time."

Another pause.

"Please hurry, this is a matter of some urgency." She glances up at me with the trace of something glinting in her eyes. "Getting his supervisor," she murmurs. She hands me the completed "Order to Remove Government Property." I look it over, trying to read the fine blurred print, as the paper trembles in my unsteady hand. It's real. I didn't see her invent all this just now, she must have dug it out from somewhere. This is real. I can believe in it.

He must have hurried because a loud voice comes quickly through the line, asking what's all this about a remote-control car. I can hear his hard phone voice from a distance. While she tells him, she uses scissors to trim out a small rectangle of paper, and begins to work that into some kind of official form or document with the black-inked quill.

"What's the license plate number?" I hear him say.

I grab for a sheet of paper to scribble on, but she waves me away.

"That's classified," she says.

"Well—what's the make of the car?"

"Also classified."

"What about the registration and serial number?"

"Sir, the vehicle in question is a prototype and the information you're requesting is of a highly sensitive nature. If you can verify that you towed a red sedan of no identifiable make or model from near the intersections of Ocean and Colorado, we can send a team down to recover the vehicle immediately. Now do you or do you not have such a vehicle in your custody?"

They do. We go out to the van and stop at a convenience store for a disposable razor. I shave in the restroom of the passport-photo store. Without lather, like always. I like shaving to be painful, so that I do it less. It's not good for you, cutting away body parts. But like the soldiers of the Roman legions, I can't have a beard some enemy might grab hold of and yank on.

My hair is no problem, short like always. The small rectangular document is my U.S. Naval Intelligence ID card, complete with ornamental scrollwork on the borders and tiny baroque anchors in the corners. We do the thumbprint on the back with an old carbon off a credit card receipt she digs from the trash, and stick it all together in a drugstore plastic-lamination machine. We find me a dark blue polyester suit and tight black shoes in a Goodwill store. I say the shoes are too tight and she explains that's better, I'll have that impatient shifty-footed look and the OPG guys will be inclined to fuck with me less.

Finally in a murky dusk we head out across the crisscrossed maze of surface streets toward the coast. We stop and start and stop. It's endless. Every block has a stoplight. The blocks go on and on forever in every direction. There must be more stoplights than rats in the city. More stoplights than flies. More stoplights than people. It's a city of stoplights. Of, by and for the stoplights. Who's in charge here?

The shoes are too small for my feet. No matter how I put my feet they can't get comfortable. It gets tighter and tighter. The seat is uncomfortable as hell. There's no room in the van to sit comfortably. There's no room in the city, to move comfortably. You can't shrug your shoulders without bumping into someone, or something. Like a stoplight. It gets harder and harder to breathe.

"Can't we get on the freeway or something?"

"Rush-hour," she says without looking over. "This is faster. Believe it or not."

"Christ!"

"I don't like surface streets any more than you do," she says. She glances over at me and sees me sweating. She nods.

85

"That's good," she says. "You want that irritated look."

"You really think this is going to work?"

She frowns. "Why wouldn't it?"

"The documents are great and everything, I can hardly believe they're not real. Except, of course, that I saw you make them. And also, I'm pretty certain I never joined any naval intelligence organization." I pause, and think about it. "Fairly certain, anyway. But this OPG outfit, they've got to have their procedures and everything."

"Fuck their procedures. We don't fit any of their categories."

"What if they call somebody?"

"Who are they going to call? We're a highly classified unit. I don't imagine they have the home number for the Secretary of the Navy."

"Well, I guess it's worth a shot."

"A shot?"

"If it doesn't work out I can always hire on with the OPG as a tow-truck driver."

She locks up the brakes and yanks us over to the curb, swerving and squealing and smoking the tires. We lurch to a stop and sit staring at each other. Her nostrils flare with her breathing. She says, suddenly, "What is this shit? It already worked, it's a fact, you're naval intelligence, don't you get that? This is not a game, shithead. This is your job. Don't you know who you are?"

"Sure. No problem."

"'Cause if you don't, then get your ass out of the van right now. What do you think this is. We're not here to fuck around. You're the one who was talking about art. So make up your mind, whether you're with us or against us. You're the one who was talking about no compromise, no regret.

You're the one who shot off your fat mouth."

"All right. All right." She sits there staring at me with her fingers drumming on the steering wheel. "Come on, drive."

She pulls out into the headlighted traffic and mutters something I can't make out.

"Shit," I say. "I never used to need any lectures on conviction."

"Just concentrate," she says.

"Nor on concentration, either."

She nods, slowly. "Some people lose only their dreams here. That's not so bad."

"What do you mean not so bad, it's death."

"Maybe they don't know how lucky they are. If they lose the dream they lose the memory of it too. So they never know they're missing anything. Dreams are merciful that way."

"I don't believe there's any such thing as a happy fool," I say.

"What does happiness have to do with it?"

"Everything. Happiness is just a word, for something else. Something way different. Something important."

"I don't know what you're talking about," she says. I watch her face in the shifting glare of the oncoming head-lights. The pearly mask never shifts, never changes.

"Sure you do."

"Fuck you! What do you know about dreams? Nightmares are dreams too you know. I was lying just then—no dream is ever forgotten, they all leave their residue, maybe it's only a ringing in your ears or a taste in the back of your throat. People think they've lost their dreams, they haven't lost shit. They can always have them back. All they have to do is wish. Want something they never had. It's the others who are in deep shit."

87

"What others?"

"Who lose themselves. Bit by bit, piece by piece."

"You just have to know when to get out," I say.

"Get out then!" she cries. It's the first time she's raised her voice, pitched higher in sudden warning and alarm. I glance over and can barely make out her profile in the darkness. "Leave," she says with her voice dropped back down to a husky whisper. "Don't bother with the car."

"What?"

"Leave now, as fast as you can. It's like you said, you have to know when to get out. I'll drop you at the bus station, the train station, the Ventura County line—that's as far as I can go."

"I can't leave without the car."

She doesn't say anything. Nobody does. I think I hear her sigh.

"It's all right," I say. "I know when to get out—as soon as I get the car back."

"What about the mission?"

"Mission?"

"You said you came here with a mission."

"Oh yeah. Sure. Two in fact. It's a dual mission. But, you know, if it's a question of survival." She doesn't say anything. "It's still art," I say. "Rudimentary, maybe. But aesthetics grows out of ethics, and ethics is rooted in survival."

She murmurs something quiet, hard to make out, I think it's "That doesn't sound so heroic."

"Might not be pretty. But it's logical." She drives in silence. "Maybe it was just a crazy dream, anyway," I say. "I mean, crazier than most."

"What dream," she says.

"Driving down the L.A. freeways at 200-plus. You know,

showing the people."

"What people?"

"Everybody. The masses."

"Don't bother, they're not worth it."

"Bullshit!"

"What makes you think they deserve it? What makes you think you have anything to show them? What makes you think these seething assholes want to know anything you might be able to tell them? You can't even remember where you parked your car."

"Hey. I can show them plenty. I'll show *you*, once I get the car and I blaze on out of here at mach point-two-five. These freeways are capable of 200 and more. Nobody realizes that. Well they're going to realize it. They're going to wake up. When I go past them with a blur and a high-whining hum, and they feel quivering through their wrists and shinbones a whole new sensation for what the word speed is really all about."

She glances over at me in the dark. I can see only the dark pools of her black-shadowed eyes, and the pale waxy luster of the skin of her cheek.

"Don't you see," I say. "There's no limit. The only limit is the one you put on it. On yourselves. If you—"

"Don't lump me with them."

"All right, OK, what I mean is, I'll be saying to them, Hey, change your mind. Just, change it. Shrug your shoulders and decide, I'm doing something different today. I'm not driving to work. I'm finding my straightaway this morning and I'm redlining this baby—and maybe you'll get somewhere up around 120, 125—who knows? So maybe your speedometer doesn't go that high. So what? You'll never know how fast you can go if you don't peg it with the pure utter intention of flying right off the top end. You go vaulting off, you transcend the schematic—and it's a new dimension. A new state. A whole different life form. An evolutionary leap. Making the first tool. Discovering fire. You just don't have any idea," and the joy and laughter bubble up out of me as the spirit of it comes over me.

"Nobody knows," I say, "the feeling, like possession—no, completeness. I'll show 'em! There's nothing like it. I mean, if it weren't for the twins, I could fly down the freeway so fast I'd dissolve into pure light. Pure essence. But of course I can't. They draw me back. I—"

"You sure it's them?" she says, "and not you?"

"Yeah I'm sure. I can't just leave like that—not unless I knew they were watching. If they could see it as it happened—wow! It's something I've got to teach 'em, show 'em, one way or another. Speed, motion, life, heat light illumination, it's all there, it's the trial by speed, it's the pinpoint focus of the timeless frozen blur, it's cold and hard as ice and fast as the streaking spinning orbits of atoms, you never know where the electron is 'cause it's nowhere and everywhere all at the same moment—that's me, on the freeway. I been preparing for this all my life, from day one of consciousness. It might only happen once. It only needs to happen once. One time, pure speed, pure motion, pure...light! That's it! I mean, my car runs on pure alcohol. What does that tell you?"

I sit back, sighing, with the warm flush pumping through me and a tingling glow tickling lightly all over my skin. "When I drive 200+ miles an hour, that's when I know I'm alive." I don't know if I say it or just know it. She doesn't say anything. Time passes, I guess. Maybe not. We drive on through the dark.

"The twins," she says.

"Yes," I sigh. "My boys."

"Where are they?"

"That's the other part of the mission—to find them."

"In L.A.?"

"Orange County."

"Uh-oh," she says.

"Why?"

"L.A. is bad—down there it's worse. A ten-thousand square-mile concentration camp. Does weird things to people. Better hope they're not too twisted."

"Well, I've got to find them."

"Sure," she says. "That should be easy."

"Easy?"

"Compared to the other—driving 200-plus on the L.A. freeways."

"I kind of had it figured the other way around. How do you track down two seven-year-olds in ten thousand square miles of tract houses?"

"Simple," she says. "Ever see the city maps they make, with a grid and plastic overlays: here's the bus routes, the freeways, smog densities, etc. etc. etc.?"

"Sure. I mean, I can imagine."

"People only have one plastic overlay in their brain at a time. Maybe only one their whole life. That's their life, on a styrene sheet. They have it all figured out. Then abruptly they're amazed to stumble across the intimation of a layer under theirs. Or, worse, over! Squashing them down. Insignificating them. Dehumanizing them, they say—and they're the ones with the styrene map in their brains."

She glances toward me, waiting I guess. "OK," I say. "So what?"

"Screw the plastic layers," she says. "You can't think that

91

way. You'll never find them. What you have to figure out is, what's under that cardboard city grid that all the plastic overlays lie on top of."

We ride on through the dark, stopping and starting and stopping, and I think about it. "What?" I say.

She sighs. "But that's the easy part. The other: 200 miles an hour on the freeway, spreading that kind of dream—in this town? Impossible."

"What do you mean, it'll be no problem. I'll find some stretches of freeway, at two or three in the morning, I don't care. Just let it thin out for a mile or two and I'll do it. I only have to show a few people, there'll be a ripple effect, it'll spread like wildfire. You'll see grandpas and truckers and UCLA girls in convertible rabbits, all doing 130-plus down the freeway."

"Right," she says. "Try finding that thinned-out mile or two."

"Come on, it's got to thin out every now and then."

"Go ahead," she says. "Try. You won't find it. Not in L.A."

"Hell, how many miles of freeway they got here? Six, seven, eight lanes wide per side. There's got to be some—"

"Eight lanes of slowly oozing parking lot. You'll be lucky to get over fifty. You feel like you're flying when you hit sixty-five. Listen, I got a master's degree on the freeway. Would've had my PhD, only I never finished the dissertation."

"I'll find it," I say. "You got to believe in something—I'll find it on my way out of town."

"Oh, sure, out in the sticks somewhere. Out toward Barstow or Hemet or Gorman. Not in L.A. proper. And what kind of mission is it, if you don't take the message to the heart? Fine, linger around the perimeter, be some buzzard-man. Nobody gives a shit, out in the sticks. Everyone's looking inward, to the center. Why do you think I'm here? Why do you think you're here? We're all looking inward inward inward always inward—for the center. Don't seem to be finding it."

I see or feel or imagine a spiralling inward, a focusing searching pattern for a center that might never have been. The shoes and the van and the city feel smaller and smaller, crushing me tighter and tighter, squeezing the air from my chest. I strain to breathe. "I'll find it," I whisper. "It's here, I know it."

"Sure you'll find it—halfway to Phoenix. Go ahead, cruise L.A. Take a tour on your way out. Rush-hour, twenty-four hours a day. Sixteen lanes packed wall to wall—gridlock. I know these freeways. I can tell you all about them. I've paid my dues. I used to love them. Not now. Maybe I do. It's love/hate. They exacted their price. I swore I'd never get on a freeway again as long as I live." The words flow from her without a seam. No passion, no pain, nothing. Words. Streaming, clear, placid as liquid air. "I stuck to the surface streets for a while. But the freeways—they get you. Lying there, reposing, sinuous and interlinked and intertwined across the breast of the land, anchored in the earth through perfect towering gray pillars, with upward-spiralling curves to suck you up and around and on—you're on! Gliding, sliding, slipping and driving on and on and on. I've watched men at the beach watching Isis, in all her million gilded forms spread across the blonde sand like an endless sexual smorgasbord—just like those men are drawn, that's how I was drawn. It's biological. Relentless, helpless—back to the freeway. Oh the wide lanes and the curves and the spirals, the pure logic, the order and symmetry—what perfect sense it all makes. Simple transitions, that somehow went and became

93

entire worlds of their own—and you go, you're drawn you're seduced you're captured, sometimes late at night, in the dark before dawn when the smog's still invisible, and you end up sitting there, you can't breathe and wish you never came. The orange sun rises and the sky turns shades of brown-streaked yellow and you're sitting there. How did I get here? Only you come again, and again. Oh it's all so logical, the plan the pattern the schematic, all etched somewhere on greasy-slick styrene pages, so purely logical. You keep talking about logic—at least you keep saying the word. Only now, somehow, you're stuck." She falters, momentarily, to pant and catch at her breath before the words come again, slightly sing-song now, almost like someone else is doing the talking. "You're not moving. You're parked, frozen in a faulted presupposition, like an unsuspected fault-line under the foundation of the freeway cloverleaf that brings each over-pass crashing down on all the rest in chaotic, logical se-quence. Or, surprise, maybe it's not a shitty premise, maybe perfect logic can screw you too, if you extrapolate and extend and extrude it far enough, purely logical, right? America, right? What does all this imply toward the system, the process, huh? So if A=A, A is either B or not B, right? And the lanes—one's moving, one's not. What does that tell you? Having a nice day? Maybe one's still and all the others are slipping backward. Sucked backward, toward what? A car spins off, berserk, slicing through lanes, through cars, people. Why? Why ask. Who wants to know. You sit there—you sit there. Hey surprise, here come some memories. Maybe they're memories you didn't count on seeing again. Memo-ries you thought you lost. It eats you. Nothing's the same, ever again. It never will be. Maybe it never was. Go ahead, stay off the freeway. Get out of L.A. Try. I dare you. We're there."

"What?"

She swerves to the curb and stops. I look at her. She nods toward the business on my right. OPG.

"Good luck," she says.

I open the door and step down and glance back in, holding the door open.

"Aristotle was wrong," I say.

She watches me and doesn't speak, doesn't move. Her pale mask with dark pools.

"Luck is inconsequential," I say. "It's for losers. But thanks anyway."

"Bullshit," she says, and drives away.

A high gate is rolled shut across the driveway. Bright white floodlights light up the gate and the fence and the shiny cold coils of razor-edged barbed wire looped across the top. Signs warn of attack dogs and armed patrols. I open a side door and step into the office. The shoes are like vices and my feet are throbbing. The stupid suit pinches my armpits and compresses my shoulders. I have to walk like a robot and hold my arms in close to keep from splitting the seams of the jacket.

A bearded guy in a tow-truck uniform sits at a cluttered desk. The room is divided by a midriff-high wall, topped with a counter. Above that, bars and a sheet of bulletproof glass separate us. There's a small divot in the glass at eye-level and a sign with an arrow pointing to it says "A .44 magnum won't cut it." At low face-level is a small round metal intercom mike that makes your voice weird. A half-oval window in the glass at countertop level is for passing money and car keys back and forth. Another sign taped to the glass above the opening tells you not to bother writing out a check. No credit cards either. A calendar on the wall over the desk shows a blonde in white mechanic's coveralls bent over the open hood of an old Corvette. She holds a handful of greasy wrenches in one hand and a smoking revolver in the other and her long sharp fingernails are deep rich red and so is the blood splattered across the glossy immaculate white underside of the raised hood. She stares out at you with huge blue eyes like you caught her in the act of something. Her coveralls are partly unbuttoned and her tits sag out and under the picture is printed, "Don't fuck around." OK. Right.

The bearded guy stands up and comes to the counter and I pull the folded "Order to Remove Government Property" from the inside breastpocket of my dark blue Goodwill suit and drop it on the counter, making him reach through the little half-oval window for it. I pull the ID card from the same pocket and glance at it to make sure of the name, then I hold it up against the glass for him to see, first the front, then the back.

"John Day," I say. "U.S. Naval Intelligence."

"Oh yeah," he mumbles, "the dayshift left a note about this one." He glances over the "Order to Remove Government Property." I get a good look at it in bright light for the first time. All the blanks labeled "Description," "ID No.," "Serial No." and such are filled in with what looks like a stamped, slanted "CLASSIFIED." At the bottom is a line authorizing the said U.S. government property to be removed by "John Day, USNI." He flips the form over. The reverse side is blank.

"OK," he says, and hands me some forms. "You'll have to sign these." He passes three forms through the oval and I begin to sign them, "John Day, USNI." "Remote-controlled, huh," he says, watching me sign.

"Apparently."

"How's that work?"

I stop in the middle of a signature and slowly glance up till I'm staring at his face.

"I beg your pardon?" I murmur.

"Uh, never mind," he mumbles, looking around behind him. He's looking for the clock on the wall.

"Let's see," he says. "That's fifty-one-fifty, plus it ain't midnight yet, so it's one day storage, that's," and he punches it up on a calculator, "fifty-eight even."

I straighten up and slip his pen into my inner breast pocket, leaving the forms lie. He crams his hand into the tiny oval and strains his fingers, reaching for them.

"What's fifty-eight even?" I say.

"I need fifty-eight bucks before I can hand over the car keys."

"There are no keys," I say. "And the vehicle in question is not a car."

"Uh, not a car?"

"ROV," I say. "I thought my superior made it clear over the telephone that the OPG had improperly impounded U.S. government property."

"Yeah, well, I wasn't here."

"Check the form, I don't believe you'll find any mention of payment."

He finds the form and starts slowly reading through it, tracing haltingly down the lines with his black-rimmed fingernail.

"Let me talk to your supervisor," I say, with the throbbing gliding from my feet up into my ankles and shins.

"He's not here."

"Get him on the phone please, I'd like to talk to him."

He consults a list of numbers and dials one. We wait. I

stand still, staring straight ahead, showing no impatience. You have all the time in the world when you're a federal agent. Nothing else matters. The world around you gets all jittery and flustered, everyone hurries, they don't want you around. They're afraid you're miked and the IRS has a wiretap on the line. You're the calm at the eye of the hurricane. He hangs up the phone. He glances toward me and shrugs. I yawn.

"He ain't answering," he says, and pushes the form to the side. "I'll buzz you through. The car—uh, I mean the ROV—it's near the back on the left." He reaches for a doorbell-style button on the countertop on his side of the glass, and nods toward the door in the back wall.

I glance that way. "What about the dogs," I say.

"Oh it's cool," he says. "They got stolen."

I go to the door, he buzzes and I open it. "Just drive toward the gate, it'll automatically open," he calls.

I step out without speaking or turning back. My feet numbly throb. The door closes itself. The lot is big and crammed with cars. I find mine where he said. We're not blocked in. The red covering is gritty and scratched and nicked so I peel it back. The white underneath is already scarred so I pull that off too. The blue shows a few nicks so I strip that away. The red leaves a bad taste in my mouth, the car was red when they stole it from me. We need a change. I peel it off. Now we're clean and white and glossy. I pull off the Yukon plates and replace them with Delaware. It only takes a few seconds with wingnuts on the bolts. The slogan on the plates matches the car: "First In Freedom."

I slip in behind the wheel and feel its smooth tight control. It's the old type wheel with deep notched finger-grips clear around on the underside. There's no chrome on it and no provision for a horn. No need to let anyone know we're coming. We'll be past and gone before anyone knows we were there.

My feet are too numb to feel the pedals. I yank off the shoes and toss them out the window. Then the jacket. With it goes the ID card. Don't need to lug around a card telling everyone who I am. Whether it happens to be right or not. And who knows, whether life imitates art or vice versa. So watch out. Remember, even thoughts have substance. In fact, real life and real art are the same thing. But how many people ever have any experience of either? Or rather, both. It, I mean. This. I know even as I ditch it that someday she'll be famous and her artwork will be worth millions. But hey, what are millions worth? So I just threw a fortune out the window. Good.

I reach under the dash and press the spring-loaded toggle switch and she fires up with the old familiar rumble. It's been years since I felt that warm deep muttering life throbbing up through the seat of my pants. I press on the gas with my toe, lightly, and the rumble flutters through the baffled muffler and the torque tilts us slightly, to the right. Now all we're missing is Atticus, solemn and smiling across at me from the navigator's seat. I switch on the lights and drive for the gate. It opens, like he said. We're back on the streets.

We drive in a straight line till we hit a freeway. I don't know the name or number. I flip the switch that opens the headers, bypassing the muffler. We hit the on-ramp at forty and the engine is barking and roaring out through the wide black-anodized pipes just behind the front wheels and in front of the doors. By the time we curve up onto the raised causeway we're pushing 70, the Gs press me against the door and I stretch her up toward triple digits with ease and calm and laughter bubbling up from somewhere deep behind my chest. The stretched feeling in my face is from grinning.

Then, rising up level with the freeway, the on-stretching mosaic of flashing bright-red lights comes rushing at us headlong and I stand hard on the brakes, locking up all four wheels. We drift right with just the beginning of a spin and I let off and we sail between the stopped traffic and the concrete retaining wall with inches to spare on either side. We glide down the blacktopped shoulder, braking sanely, and as the shoulder narrows down on an overpass we angle left and force a gap, wedging our way in and inserting ourselves into the stream of nerds.

Where the hell they all think they're going? We go with them, hoping to find out. We're so tight-packed that we don't see a battered Volkswagen fender until we're hard upon it. There's no time to brake or swerve—luckily we're going so slow that we clump up and over with no more of a jolt than you get bouncing over a speed bump. The freeway is littered with blowing trash. Old newspapers and torn plastic bags flutter up and stick against your grill, suffocating your radiator and burning up your engine if your luck is down. Or they snag on your windshield wipers and blind you for tortured fractions of seconds, while anything and everything could be lurching to a stop only inches in front of your bumper. There must be an open garbage truck somewhere ahead, gradually launching its load into the swirling up-drafts. I keep looking for it.

The barking guttural exhaust from our open headers draws glances. We stand out in the herd—that's not good. I close them, routing our exhaust through the heavily baffled muffler system Atticus designed. We don't watch the signs (I don't believe in them either), going by instinct. We're swept in endless curves and loops and swooping spirals and nothing ever changes. Never getting over forty-five, shunted from one freeway to the next and knowing—no, believing—that perseverance alone will get us out, eventually. How long you willing to wait? To persevere, that is. We poke along. Like she said, an oozing parking lot. I weep behind the wheel, seeing the wide smooth concrete speed-ramp and knowing what I could do with it, what any of us could do with it—only we can't. We're all just nerds in the herd. Members of a slow stampede, panicking gradually. Each at his or her own pace. For some it takes years. For others, less. And I always thought everything happened fast here, here near the center of the center. Apparently not. Oh, the patience of bovine human, requiring no shepherds, no cowboys and no packs of gaunt coyotes to keep them in line. Only concrete abutments. And stock options. Credit cards. Christmas, Easter, the Fourth of July. Retirement. Pension plans. I'm having trouble breathing, the air comes in shallow panting snatches. There's nothing here for me—for either of us. It isn't the smog that makes my chest ache. The crowd closes in tighter around us, the cars are bumper to bumper and door to door. On the day they doled out patience I must've been out of town. Some people learn some lessons and some learn others. Some never learn. A few cars in front of us the back door of a van swings open and someone chucks out a dead dog. There's no room to swerve. If you brake hard someone's going to drive through your rear window. Nobody brakes. The cars ahead jolt over the body. So do we.

So all right, maybe there is no quick way out. We swirl around and around, sometimes the loops and curving arcs are large, sometimes small. Each time I expect a new vista, clear and open horizons sprawling out every which way, with the dense lights thinning gradually and stretching out toward the hinterland. If there's no fast way, we'll find a slow one. There's got to be a slow way. Dear God, let there be some way out.

Then to the right, jutting up through the smoking sky, I spot the concrete whitewashed Matterhorn. It's illuminated in a stark shadowless orangey light. Almost a dark or invisible light—it's the shadows that make light light. This is the only thing I know about Orange County: it's where Disneyland is. And, of course, the twins. Orange County. This is what they'll think of when they remember childhood. Hell. They're around here somewhere. Somewhere.

I remember the styrene maps she said people fasten their lives to, inside their brains. What's that about? Just keeping things clear, maybe. Keeping your eyes open. Not getting trapped and entangled in the spidery web of neatly drawn lines on anyone's blueprint. Especially your own. I look around as we creep along the orange and rose-lit freeway. My eyes snag on one thing, then another. The more you look, the less you see. Damn this clutter! The skyline packed with marmalade lights and man-made things, the land packed with seething rumbling freeways aiming nowhere, the freeways packed with drones in cars moving so slow they must commonly forget where it is they set out to go long before they ever get there. At the very least, they're bound to forget why.

Clear out, all of you! Go on, and leave me my lonely stretch of freeway, I'm only asking for one clear lane for three or so miles—I'll settle for two and a quarter. With a solitary deserted off-ramp winding down to a little clapboard house among the orange and lemon groves. The air is scented with orange blossoms and the honeybees thump against the windshield. My sons in a yard with a sandbox and a rusting swing-set. Maybe in this climate it wouldn't be rusting. Is that my childhood or theirs? Maybe seven is too old for a sandbox and swing-set. Kicking a football then, taking turns being the kicker and the tee, kicking field goals over the swing-set. Or was that my brother and me? Wearing miniature baseball mitts and practicing their pitching, throwing old tennis balls at a rectangle chalked on the garage door. Now and then nearly hitting the kitchen window twenty feet to the left.

Is it too much to ask? It's a normal enough vision, nothing exotic, nothing bizarre. Doesn't it exist any more, anywhere in America? All this clutter! But no, that's not the problem. It's not the clutter—it's the asking. Too much to ask? Damned right. Why you asking? Ask for the slightest tiny thing, and it's already way too much. Remember, this is America. Nobody got here by waiting for an invitation to come. By the time you get around to asking, you've already lost. Sorry. Hey, why be sorry? Deal with reality. Live every moment. There's no time for sorrow.

We're shunted onto another freeway, aiming right. We pass the burning hulk of a car shoved off onto the shoulder. Nobody's around. The fire flares fitfully and as we roll by I catch a whiff of the poisonous cancer smell of burning vinyl. We spiral inward onto another freeway. It goes on and on. Like a play with no intermission, that just goes on till it stops. Then still another freeway. And then it gradually dawns on me, that some plays might never end. And I imagine the horror, greater than that of dying, of having to go on and on living forever. In fact, I'm not changing from one freeway to another, and another, and another and so forth—because there is only one freeway. It's all one Great Freeway. One organism, one entity, one interconnected and intertwined and intertwisted whole. If it's one vast organism spreading across the length and breadth of the continent and the earth, then L.A. might be the curving twisting intestine. The bowel, maybe. If so, it's constipated as hell. Congealed and bloated and distended and likely to burst, spewing rot and infection and decay into every little pocket of haven and refuge across the face of the land. And, if this is the way it is, what does that make us?

It's obvious "The Freeway" is one whole entire thing, of many parts. There's evidence. Proof. It's logical. Listen. The distinctions they try to make between the different stretches are so forced, so arbitrary. Who can say where one ends and another begins? When two merge it sometimes becomes one, sometimes the other, and other times a new entity entirely. There's no rational pattern behind any of that. It's all pretense.

But that's only circumstantial evidence. Here's the clincher: before I stopped believing in signs, I noticed that every freeway in and around L.A. has both a name and a number. Now if it's working, if you really know where it is and what it's for, if you have the total clinical overview and rational perspective, then you only need one clear, simple, definitive means of identification. But this is just the problem, it's not definitive. Nobody's really sure. They're groping. Sure we'll give it a number. Aw what the hell, let's throw in a name too, just for good measure. Maybe somebody'll figure it out. But then you take a closer look at the names and the numbers, and none of them make any sense either. Believe me, I've done research. And the last time I checked, the San Diego Freeway didn't come within a hundred miles of San Diego. See, it's just not logical.

And then, even worse, right away it becomes obvious that the most intricate and convoluted stretch of freeway on earth—L.A.—wouldn't be the intestine after all, but rather the brain. This is much, much worse. Because it just isn't working. And because the contorted and knotted circuits and channels and conduits of any brain are virtually endless. This oozing parking lot might go on forever, and I might never find my way out.

This is almost enough to make me get off the freeway. It's the only way out. But then—surface streets! We roll fitfully on, slouched over the wheel staring at the flashing brakelights ahead, and as we pass each off-ramp the muscles in my shoulders and arms twitch and tremble, and threaten to yank the wheel to the right and spiral us down into yet another version of hell.

But from inside me rises something firmer. Not loud, at first—but strong. I don't even know what it is. Just something contrary, somehow, to the way I felt before.

And somebody somewhere seems to be saying, So what is all this, after all, about having to get out? What's the hurry? You got everything all wrapped up here and you're ready to head out already? You just got here, man. You already learned everything you got to know? Done all the things you came to do? Came, saw, and conquered, huh? Sure, right. That's so fucking swell, man. I'm glad for you. I really am. At least now you know what you're made of. Now you can see how tight you're really wound. No more lifetime of fantasy and illusion. Been nice knowing you. You came, you saw, you took a big dump. And you didn't even hang around long enough to see all that much. Probably set some kind of a record, for panning out in the bigtime. You sucked canal water. Congratulations. You're not the first. Relax, no big deal. You won't be the last. Who cares?

So all that before: no compromise, consequences only matter to wimps, will and decision and the power of adamant truth and focus and righteousness—all that was only talk, right? Idle conversation to offset the eerie silence in the waiting room. Words, filling your bored imagination, distracting you while you're waiting to die. Spewed into a bored vacant world. Trying to make a sound that's somehow different, but isn't.

But everything that was true then is still true now, right? Still immersed in shit and surrounded by distraction, digression, dissipation. What else is new? So this new attitude, this retreat—is this a reaction to a world wallowing in bullshit, or a result of getting caught up in it?

Before, I always kept myself separate. And now, suddenly I feel the body blows, the left jabs, and I'm all distracted watching for the left hook. Maybe I'm just scrambling to bail out of the ring before the Sunday punch comes barreling down that dotted white line, straight into the front of my grill at mach point-two-five.

Always been so immune to the wallowing world, Atticus and I. Laughing at the spectacle of a world choking on its own fumes. We were always aloof. How much sense does it make to sit around suffocating in your own farts? About fifteen million people in greater Los Angeles think it makes fine sense. We used to think it was hysterically funny. Half the people in the fourteen western states. But up close it's not so funny. It's terrifying. Up close like this, it overwhelms you.

Never had time for this kind of bullshit before, for fear or terror or doubts. The disintegration was always outside, sometimes completely surrounding us—but never inside. So immune, I dared to come to the thickest densest core of it, the center of the center, packed tighter than a collapsed star where a teaspoonful weighs ten thousand pounds. I *knew* I could handle the Gs. No problem.

So if you never had time for it before—the qualms, the quandary, the disintegration—why do you suddenly have time for it now? Now, of all moments. Never been closer to the twins. Never been closer to the center. And suddenly you're so desperate, so eager to give up. Infected by the doubts of others. When all you need is that one clear stretch, two and a quarter miles, one lane wide. We've never believed in odds. Statistics have nothing to do with it. They're just not logical—ask Atticus. Seem strange, believing in logic and miracles at the same time? But strangeness, Mr. Johnson, is perfectly normal around here. And of course it would be even stranger if there weren't miracles than if there were.

Maybe you forgot that there's a war happening. Only one way to win a war: by not fighting in it. If you know any dances start dancing instead. If not, then sure, line up. Go ahead. The firing squad's got plenty of spare bullets and they're tired of shooting only the deserters. They're ready. It's their job and they're doing it. Meanwhile, who's doing yours? When the Robbers of Attention start robbing your self, it's not the robbers' fault. It all comes down to a simple question: Can you cope with this? But that's not the real question: Where the hell's all this doubt coming from? Who's in control here? Control? Who the hell wants to know?

We're not finished here yet. We came on a mission. It's all about heroism. You're not a good guy unless you're good. And if you're not a good guy, you're a bad guy. It's black and white. So make up your mind. We made up ours, like everybody does. And we're sticking to it. We'll do our best.

We have to, otherwise we'll never know how good our best really is. Nobody ever said it was going to be easy. Are we Americans or aren't we? It's bound to be tough, you should know that going in. The tougher the better. Otherwise every jerk would get there ahead of you. Would've got used up and trampled over and worn out several generations back. Hopefully, it'll be nearly impossible—otherwise it's hardly worth the bother. Besides, we're Americans. The last or the first— doesn't matter. It's not in the American soul, the American constitution, to give up just because it happens to not be easy. That's just all the more reason to kick ass.

And then, of course, there are the twins. Can't leave them here without first giving them some clue, what it means to really be an American. I can't abandon them to *this*. It's caricature-land. Home of Disneyland, remember? I've got to find the twins.

I don't know whether time is passing. Remember, I don't believe in time, either. The lane we're following, staring straight ahead, is sucked off to the right, swirled around and down, and we're off the freeway.

We drive through a dim orange and rose dawn across concrete shattered by generations of heavy trucks. We see them, parked by delivery docks with their rears yawning open. Dark silent men work by hand or forklift to fill them, or to empty them. Big industrial yards lie abandoned, fenced off and weed-grown. Signs are in a foreign language. Spanish, I guess. The walls and fences are spray-painted with square backward-leaning letters in red and black.

We swerve right onto a sidestreet and pull to the curb. We park in front of a shut-down warehouse loading dock. The corrugated strip-steel door is spray-painted in another language. Malaysian, maybe, or Maori. Maybe it's hieroglyphics. The harder I stare, the more blurred they look. I shut down the engine and slide low in the driver's seat, tilting my head back and using the seatback for a pillow.

A pink glow comes over the world. Through half-closed eyes I watch a blurred geometry fill the horizon. The block is filled with precise lines and curves: the street, edges of sidewalks and buildings, telephone poles, wires. Cracks in the pavement, cracks in the walls, cracks in the sky. Everything is precise, and blurred. I let everything be how it is. Shapes mingle, separateness dissolves and emerges again in new combinations, dissolves and re-emerges, dissolves and re-emerges. It all continues. A chunk of building and of sky, of street and sidewalk, of pole and wires and wall. Then the parts of a single whole stop having to be contiguous. This is more wonderful. No, more real. I think, How true: a jigsaw puzzle is so much more interesting before it's put together. Not only in what it could or might be. Rather, in how it looks. Lying in the box or on the floor, scattered across the yard, dropped from an airplane into thick woods—each oddly cut piece, each shape, what it is, not needing to be squeezed into any larger pattern. Scattered like gems through a forest. Precious as antique coins, raining down upon the city like hailstones. Sit in your car on any quiet street in the predawn, and through half-closed eyes watch the puzzle crumble. Only, remember: the before and after shots of Humpty Dumpty don't ever look quite the same.

A sound comes against the glass. By my face, on the left. I know then that there was a sound from the right, before, from the warehouse. Something looms in the left window. An eye of mine wanders that way. An alabaster mask, tinted pink in the cheeks. It's talking. I roll down the window.

We're blocking the loading dock. I fire up and roll ten feet ahead. She rolls alongside at a distance of two yards, looking the car over.

"Who drew the lines?" she says.

"Lines."

"The car."

"Nobody drew any lines. We're not into lines. We just shaped it, Atticus and I." I shut off the engine and get out and run my fingers across the glossy white-plastic surface. Below, somewhere below, how many layers deep I don't know, is the smooth varnished wood finish. Cold-molded, strip-planked like a racing yacht. Atticus did that part, the finishwork. We had dreamed once of doing an inlay. He never said anything more about it and I never asked. I only showed up in time to help him plaster on some layers of adhesive, redwhiteblueredwhiteblue and so forth. "Atticus, mostly," I say. "I guess he was the brains behind it, really. It was my idea, and he made it work. He was logical. I just went by instinct. He navigated, I drove."

She nods or seems to, and doesn't say anything. She turns and wheels toward her van. "If you help load, you can come if you want," she calls to me, and hoists herself in, and collapses the chair and hauls it in after her.

I vault up onto the loading dock. The steel door is half-raised and just inside are objects of unusual form. I can't describe them. When you move, they change. When you don't move they change too. The van backs in and the rear doors swing open and I carry them into the back, six in number. I close the rear van doors and move to pull down the corrugated steel door, and she calls back not to bother. I leave it open and jump down and climb in the passenger seat.

"Nobody'll go in," she says.

"How do you know?"

She shrugs. "Who cares? Besides, there's the inscriptions." She glances across at me, just for a moment, with something in her face that might be puzzlement. "You have a good sense of direction."

I almost say, "Do I know you?"

I don't. We drive (by freeway) and the land stretches on forever. I look out the window and it's the same. I look out later and it's the same again. What would the styrene map of this place look like? This sheet shows all the freeways. This one shows the locations of all the 7-Eleven stores. This one's the gas stations. The shopping malls. The banks, the stop-lights, the instalubes, the mass murderers, the drive-by shootings. You can put everything on styrene sheets and lay them all over the cardboard grid and then you know every-thing about everything. Except, what's under the cardboard grid?

"Where are we?" I say.

"Orange County."

We spin off the freeway and meander among surface streets. Then we turn into a school parking lot and stop along the red curb in front of the office.

"How old are your sons?" she says.

"Seven. No, eight."

"Grade three?"

"That sounds right."

She unloads her wheelchair and lowers herself into it. I go with her into the office. A tall and thin secretary with gray hair on top of her head looks up.

"Can I help you?" she says.

"Yes. I'm Janice Day, I have some sculptures I'd like to show to your third-grade class.

The woman stands up, staring at her, and backs toward a

closed door. "Could you wait here a minute please? Just a moment, I'll be right back."

She goes in and a few seconds later comes back out, following a bustling younger woman. "My God, it is you," says the younger woman, stopping just inside the room with her face going slack and amazed. Then she remembers herself, and smiles and steps forward. "Miss Day, I'm pleased to meet you," she says and shakes hands. The artist nods a little, with her eyes closed and her head tilted slightly to one side, like she can barely stand the formalities. She holds her hand out, limply, and lets the principal shake it once or twice. "Would you like to have the students assemble in the gymnasium?"

"No, thank you, just the third-graders, in their class-room," she says with great patience.

"Very well, if you wish. When would be a good time?"

"Now, please."

"Yes of course, that can be arranged, in fact, it is, isn't it," she says turning to the thin older woman, who nods.

"He'll carry them." She nods toward me.

"Do you need any help?" asks the secretary. "I can call Mr. Paul."

"No thanks, I can get it."

"I'll show you the way," says the principal.

We follow her outside. The artist stops. "I'll go ahead," she says to me. "Bring them in one at a time."

"Room nine," says the principal. "Around the corner to the right."

I carry the pieces in one at a time. The artist sits in the left rear corner of the room, saying nothing. The teacher sits at her desk in front, attentively, watching with her hands clasped and both forearms resting on the desktop. The children watch as I bring in all six, laying them on a long table in the back. Nobody speaks. I sit in the right rear corner in a tiny third-grader's chair and watch.

Finally one little girl says, pointing, "What's that?"

Nobody says anything. The artist clears her throat. "I don't know," she says finally, in a hollow voice.

Nobody speaks until another little girl says, "Can we move?"

Again silence. And now finally, in a quiet voice, "You can do anything you want."

Remember, I don't believe in time. Only now nobody else does either. They stare at the six pieces, at her, at me. I watch them. These are eight-year-olds. They're not babies any more. Still, in a way. The tiny chairs and tables. I don't know, I can't remember. I haven't changed. I slept with a tiger and a bear until I was twelve. Then I put them on a shelf, and apologized to them in whispers. If I still had them I'd probably still talk to them. I still feel the same. I just look different. I'm like you, like everyone: I didn't grow up, I just got older.

A bell rings and outside is filled with the running and shouting of children. Nobody moves. We all stare and outside it grows quiet.

"Class, it's time for lunch," says the teacher. It's quiet again. We all stare. She says it again and stands up. The children blink and look around and stand up too, looking at each other like they just came up from underwater. Or maybe the opposite. Soon we're alone in the room, the artist and I and the six pieces. The teacher had said something, I don't know what, and left. I look at the artist.

"Let's go," she says.

We stop at two more schools that day, and more on the

following days. While she drives, she begins to ask questions. Only a few. A very few.

She wants to know about speed. I tell her how for me it came in three stages. First the skateboards, where I hit a record 37 m.p.h. on my home-built 58-inch speedboard. Then skis. Nobody measured our speed up there. We lived for air, and they say that terminal velocity in freefall is 120 miles per hour. I guess our top speed was somewhere shy of that. Third came cars. At somewhere over 200, somewhere between Moses Lake and Ephrata, numbers stopped mattering. We found that other way of being. I mentioned it before. I do my best to tell her, how it all slows down and you get to experience firsthand the reality of Heisenberg's Uncertainty Principle, stability in flux, and vice versa—the searing speed in frozen motion. It seems like maybe she understands. Who knows? She probably understands something. Whether it has anything to do with what I'm talking about is a whole other question. I tell her, I guess we've always been pushing the limit, Atticus and I. I tell her, I guess we always will.

You used to hear a lot about time capsules but they're out of fashion now. Probably because everyone thought that everything everyone else put in them was stupid. So let's just go out to any stretch of the L.A. freeway, scoop up two hundred and forty yards' worth of detritus, and lock that up in a titanium orb for five thousand years. That'll tell 'em everything they ever wanted to know.

You could stock entire franchises of museums from what you find scattered along the freeway. Everything that modern society produces ends up strewn across the hard delineated concrete. You bump over the flattened specimens or spot them intact on the blacktop shoulder—where the shoulder hasn't been gobbled up for additional laneage.

Dogs, cats, possums. Sometimes whole, sometimes in parts and pieces. Hubcaps representing every artistic taste. Mattresses. Visqueen. Rope and cordage. Every imaginable car, motorcycle, and bicycle part. Celery, broccoli, cauliflower. Once I thought I saw splattered tomato, but it wasn't vegetable. It was animal. Human goes under animal.

Your timing has to be very precise to find humans strewn across the freeway. They're quick about stopping traffic and scooping up the remains before it's all splattered and pounded away to nothing. See there's a danger in leaving human bodies on the freeway. It might be too big a shock. It might wake somebody up.

Saturday (I guess) and it's raining. We head out onto the freeway, looking for two miles of straightaway. Don't find it. The place is a mess. We come close to getting nailed twice. Once swerving to miss the hood of a car lying crumpled in our lane. An upcoming geek brakes too hard and nearly slams into us from behind—I know he's coming and pull over onto the skinny shoulder to let him smear past and cream the car ahead. The second time we brake hard and swerve to miss a car spinning out on the slick pavement. They lose it trying to miss a rumpled car door lying in their lane. They go off the shoulder and down the slope into the shrubbery and that's the last we see of them.

Both times we're in complete control. They're not. In Seattle, the traffic wigs out when it snows. In L.A. all it takes is a little rain. Somehow we make it back to the warehouse, in the dark.

Sunday (I guess) I'm lying on a straw mat on top of a woven Indian blanket on the smooth concrete floor with the rain pounding down outside. The designs on the blanket probably mean something important. I lie on my back and watch the shadows and gloom above. Around me I feel cool dry empty space stretching away into the distance. I don't hear her quiet rubber wheels rolling across the smooth concrete.

"Come with me," she says from close beside me. I stand up and follow her. She stops by a four-poster bed with wrought-brass headboard and footboard. The heavy antique coverlet hangs just to the floor. I'm aware of a nearby window, suspended in space, a wavery soot-streaked pane with the rain crashing down beyond.

The old bed is too high for her to hoist herself onto it. She glances up to me and I lift her and set her on it near the center. She wears a white robe that matches her skin and she pulls this back off her shoulders and off. I sit on the bed and look at her strong chest, where an eagle is tattooed in black, about to land with claws extended, talons gripping downward toward her belly and abdomen, and looking down that way too. The wings arch up and outward and their tips encircle her small tan-colored nipples.

She watches me looking. "I can make one for you," she says. "If you want."

"Yes," I say, "only I can't."

"You can," she says. "Yours could be better, I wouldn't have to work in a mirror."

"No," I say. "It's religious. Because if I ever burn, I have to burn clean, like my car. No impurities. See, I don't wear any jewelry."

"You wear clothes though."

"Clothes that burn, none that melt. No oil," I say, and take them off. I sit in front of her and we look at each other. We're both naked. Her legs are folded and very thin. She sits a little to the side, holding herself up with her left arm. I lean toward her to kiss her. She turns her face to the side.

"No," she says, "I'm not ready. Not for that."

"All right. What are you ready for?"

"Anything else."

"What can you do?"

"Anything you want."

She reaches with her right arm and catches me around the shoulder and neck, and with her left re-arranges her legs.

"All right," she says.

"How far down can you feel?"

"I can feel everything."

"You can?"

"Feeling is an attitude," she says, "not a thing."

Later she tells me, "Remember, everything still works." A pink flush comes into her face and, soon after, she holds herself tightly against my chest and shakes with deep sobs. Her tears trickle down my breast. This is the first time I've seen her cry. Or laugh. Or smile even. This is the first time I see her.

At twilight the rain is over and I go outside to the car. It's a good time to head for the freeway, with the pavement rinsed clean and the car washed slick and glossy from the fresh rainwater.

It isn't. The car is covered with streaks and whorls of fine black grit. It's filthy. How can anyone survive here, where the rain doesn't cleanse, but rather shits on you? I have to get out. The sooner the better.

I don't.

The problem is, the worse it gets the more reason there is to stay. Both missions become that much more important. The stakes keep spiralling upward. Oh well. Would you really want it any other way? Maybe. Do you ever really reach a limit, or is that all just fitful imagination?

We visit more elementary schools. I could tell you how long this goes on only it's hard to keep track of something you don't believe in. Once we pass a motorhome with Idaho plates pulled over on the shoulder of the freeway. Famous Potatoes. A woman with short gray hair is dragging an old man out the open rear door and down the steps, feet-first. Snowbirds heading south. His arms trail and his head bounces on each of the steps going down. She lets the body lie and climbs back up and goes inside. The cars flow past and so do we. In the side mirror I see her merging back into the stream behind us.

I look from the mirror to the sculptress. She's staring ahead and gripping the wheel. Her hands are strong and her knuckles are white.

"How's that for togetherness?" I say.

She doesn't seem to move. She might be shaking her head, slowly. I might be imagining it.

"Is there any reason," I say, "why you roll silently away into the shadowy distance every evening, and I wake up before dawn on the hard concrete, alone again? Or, still?"

"Does there have to be a reason?"

"Maybe there should be."

"Do you care?"

"I guess I'm supposed to say I don't." I think about it, or try to. I wonder why I brought it up. I like waking up alone before dawn on the smooth concrete. What is it I want? Solitude, I guess. Inner solitude. Is that the same thing as inner peace? A union that only goes skin-deep, maybe. To be able to be alone, and yet not have to be. Now I have the opposite. Always cluttered on the inside, crowded on the outside. Maybe I want to touch without being touched. Or vice versa. Maybe I don't want to have to think about it anymore. Maybe I don't have a clue and I just happen to be here listening, while somebody else is carrying on a conversation with my mouth that I think has something to do with me.

"I guess I do," I say.

"You have your mission," she says, "and I have mine. Neither of us needs the distraction."

"Is it that arduous, do you think?" Yes. "That relentless?" Of course it is. Who's asking? "You can't pause a moment, rest maybe—"

She glances across at me, her eyes are hot, she glares. "Rest? I can rest after I'm dead—maybe."

Jesus. I know that. What's going on? I'm just tired sometimes. It's too crowded in here, too many of us pushing different ways all at once. No, it's not rest I want. The opposite. I just want to be light. Want to be unloaded somehow, unburdened. Uncluttered. I used to be light, I was nimble. It wasn't that long ago. I was quick then. How do you find something when you don't know what it is exactly? Will you know when you see it, if you don't know what you're looking for? Let's hope so. Let's hope, at least. We don't talk much. Don't have to. We each have our mission. Of course, they're two different missions. That's inevitable. But in the meantime we've caught a glimpse of one another. Like seeing somebody in the next car on the freeway. Sometimes that's all you have to know—that one glance. We happen to be in the same car for a while. Don't get me wrong, it's more than a carpool. More than symbiotic even. Synergistic, maybe. Two bodies can occupy the same place at the same time after all. Maybe even three. Time will tell. If it hasn't already.

At one school a young woman working as a student teacher helps me carry the pieces back to the van. During the three round-trips she says she saw me watching the kids and I tell her Yes, I'm looking for my sons. She says maybe her father can help, he knows everybody.

In the van on the freeway I ask the artist if she wants to come.

"When?" she says. This evening. She frowns. She asks their name and I tell her. "Oh they're French," she says.

I don't know.

"You know the French," she says. "Conglomerate people. I hate France. They're neither of the north nor the south but they claim the attributes of both. I had the best time of my life in France—well maybe the second best—but I'll never go back. I'm working on a project," she says. "I can't go tonight."

I've never seen her work on any project.

"Oh one other thing," she says. "If you fuck don't tell me about it."

I go where Maja says. She meets me outside a tall apartment building. A man in uniform guards the front. He's not there to open the door and help you in, he's there to quiz you and keep you out. Luckily he asks Maja the questions instead of me.

She goes to an elevator and stands waiting but I explain to her, It's a religious thing, I have to use the stairs. She comes with me. Her father isn't here, she says. This is on the way, her friends live here, he's a reporter and maybe he can help too.

We wait in their apartment looking out at the big dark view. The two women have drinks. The wife, a redhead, drinks scotch. Maja has something else, I don't know what.

They don't have mescal so I'm not even tempted. I wouldn't drink anyway but I would be tempted.

Finally he gets home. The reporter. He has a drink too. I'm going crazy, waiting. He asks what I know about the twins and their mother and I ask, What do you mean? I know everything, in a way. But he wants details. I know almost nothing. He shakes his head, pours another drink and suggests we all soak in a jacuzzi.

All right, at least we're going somewhere, doing something. I go crazy when I have to watch people standing or sitting around holding drinks with the ice clinking. We have to go down one floor. Politely, they all take the stairs. They carry towels. When we get there a sign says, No Nudity. Too bad. I can't go in there with clothes on. Besides, I don't believe in signs. I undress and slide naked into the warm slippery water. Nobody seems to mind. The others have cleverly worn swimsuits under their clothes.

"What the hell," says the husband. "This is California, what's a little nudity here in the land of debauchery?"

"We're all naked under our clothes," says Maja. It sounds familiar and a little stupid. She smiles at me.

"Are you debauched?" asks the redheaded wife, and cackles.

"Neither," I say.

"Oh!" says her husband. "Oh ho!" He guffaws and sinks beneath the water. He surfaces later and we all stare up at a few wet heavy stars bright enough to outshine the city. Someone is stroking my penis with their foot underwater but I don't look to see who. From somewhere below and out and down, a few blocks away maybe, comes the popping sound of gunshots, then sirens. A helicopter loiters with his spotlight stabbing down. They go away and it's quieter and the

121

husband says, gazing up from the warm pool, "It's hopping out there tonight."

"I have to go," I say and stand up.

"Yeah we really do," says Maja standing up fast, with the water streaming off her. Her wet black suit sticks to her breasts and clings to the smooth flattened curve of her belly. I pull on my clothes without drying and walk around feeling damp, like the few moist stars that throb through the thick sky overhead.

We drive west in my car to her father's house. I don't know what happened to her car or if she has one. I follow her directions through thick surface streets and finally into dark geometric drives below large evenly spaced trees. Beyond the trees squat mansions with no yards. I ask how her father could help.

"He has connections everywhere," she says. "He knows everybody, he used to be head of a studio. That's not really any big deal," she says quickly, "there're lots of former presidents of studios running around L.A."

"What do you mean, studio?"

"A movie studio," she says.

I stop where she tells me to. It's a dark shaded street. The mansions glow dimly from within. I shut off the deep-rumbling engine and we get out. The street is very quiet. From far off you hear, faintly, what might be traffic on a busy surface street. No freeway sounds reach this far. She starts up the walk toward the nearest mansion, a two-story French provincial look-alike. From across the street comes a shrill drawn-out scream. I spin around with my heart crashing in my chest. The scream came from a pink-stuccoed villa crammed between English-Tudor manor houses. Maja tugs on my arm, gently. I glance at her, she sighs and rolls her eyes a little.

"It's normal," she says. "Goes on all the time."

"It reminds me," I whisper, "of a scream I heard once. No several times. A woman was having a baby. Well, trying to."

"You know what they say. The stronger the objection to being born, the higher the incarnation."

"What? Who says that?"

She shrugs. "I don't know. Tibetans I guess."

"It's bullshit. The louder the scream, the bigger the head and the smaller the mother's pelvis. The greater the squeeze and compression on the skull and brain. The tighter the cord is wrapped around its neck."

"That's very western," she says. "Cause and effect and all." She smiles in the faint dark, and reaches and takes my hand and leads me up the walk, winding through the grass.

"I'm an American," I say.

She laughs, softly. "That's very unusual," she says.

She leads me inside. In the living room a tall calm man in his fifties stands before a living fire in the stone hearth. His straight blond hair hangs nearly to his shoulders, framing his narrow face and calm, gentle, crystal-blue eyes. On the opposite side of the hearth stands a full suit of antique armor, slightly tarnished. Slightly smaller than the man.

"My father," says Maja. "David."

We smile and shake hands. His grip is big and firm. We three go to the bar and he asks what I'll drink and I answer, Nothing right now. He fills oversize tumblers for himself and Maja and asks what brings me to L.A.

"To find my sons," I say, "and in hopes of driving over 200 miles an hour on the freeway." He asks some questions and I try to explain to him about speed.

"You ought to try getting a ride on the space shuttle," he

says. "Can you imagine the lift-off, all those Gs? Wouldn't be too tough to arrange if you knew the right people."

"No," I say. "You've got to be driving. An astronaut's like a monkey strapped to a chair, the driving's being done elsewhere. You can't be a passenger along for the ride. You're not watching a movie. You're totally alive."

"Some of the times I've felt most alive were when I was watching movies," says Maja.

I don't say anything, feeling sorry for her. I'm on the brink of telling her about control, obsession, total pure liquid concentration immune from all taint and contamination, but at the same time I feel the taint and contamination from inside myself. The fitful blur, the relentless slow dissolve of focus. Intermittent, but still incessant. The inner voids in my attention whose location and size and number I know nothing about. The something, someone, somewhere that's wracking me apart from the inside as it screams and claws its way out.

"What about the racetrack?" says David.

"What?"

"I'd think that's where you'd want to take this love of speed, out to compete with other guys who have the same passion. To measure yourself against them and see how good you really are."

"I don't believe in competition," I say.

Maja laughs. "I thought you said you're an American."

"It doesn't tell you anything about how good you really are. Even if that were important."

"Of course it does."

"It tells you how you measure up against something else. Relativism. But pure experience is what I'm talking about. Reality. Not the irreality of a little loop, with rules somebody

124

made up. It's like taking some wire mesh of tiny tiny squares and squashing it down over the top of human aspiration and potential in order to make it all fit into somebody's arbitrary categories. They make dogs and horses run around tracks too. The dogs they have to trick and the horses they have to whip—I don't know why people do it."

David laughs. "Other forms of whipping, I suppose," he says, and turns to the bar to refill his glass.

"Or tricking," says Maja. "Come on, I'll play you a song on the guitar. I wrote it myself."

She leads me through halls down one wing of the house. It's very quiet. She opens a door and we step into a bedroom. She closes the door behind me, bumps into me, hesitates a moment, and then throws her arms around my neck and gloms her mouth onto mine. I hold my mouth shut tight. Something in me pulls back—something else is tugging me forward. She opens her mouth and it's watery and hot with her breath and lips smearing across my face—but I can't part my lips. I don't try, or resist trying. It just happens that way. She breaks away, panting, and slowly moans. She's rubbing the front of her thighs and belly and breasts against me, and hooking my leg with one of hers. Her hair is in my face and we totter, about to fall. She pulls back and looks at my eyes.

"Hey," she says, "you don't have herpes or anything do you?"

"No."

"You don't shoot up or anything?"

"No."

"Me neither." She smiles. Her eyes are huge. "Wait right here." She hurries into the bathroom and rummages around, leaving the door open. "Damn!" she cries. "Where the fuck is it?"

125

"What's wrong?" I call.

"My diaphragm—I bet Claire swiped it."

I hear a woman's voice and footsteps coming down the hall. Maja runs out from the bathroom and pushes me into a big closet. "Quick, in here," she says, and closes the door.

It's black and I stumble over shoes and clothes scattered across the floor. From the bedroom I hear women's voices, Maja and another, first talking, then shouting. I wander through the racks of clothes and hangers groping for a doorknob. I find one and step out into a pitch-dark room.

"Hey, over here," whispers a voice. I go that way and trip on the edge of a big soft double bed and fall on top of a woman lying there.

"Oh, David," she murmurs, clutching me. I start to say something but feel her wet mouth groping across my cheek and I squeeze my mouth shut tight. She finds my lips and kisses them, locking onto my mouth and feeling me with her hands. "Hey!" she cries suddenly, and sits up and switches on a bedlamp. She's a Chinese woman with long straight black hair and brown-black nipples. Her big black eyes stare at me and she yanks the sheet up over her tits.

"You're not David," she says.

"I know."

"Who are you?"

"Maja brought me."

"Oh, no."

"Are you Claire?"

"No, Anna. David's secretary. Quick, go out that way, before someone comes." She points to a door, holding the plum-colored sheet over her breasts with the other hand. "Don't tell anybody, please."

I step out into a hallway and follow it toward light and

noises. A door opens beside me and I stop and look in.

"Come on in," says a tall blonde woman. I go in. It's a small bathroom. She closes the door and motions to the marble washstand. "Have a line," she says, handing me a short length of red, yellow and white-striped plastic straw.

"No thanks," I say, and smile and hand it back. "I'm a designated driver."

She takes the straw, smiling. "Good," she says. "We need more of those." She steps to the washstand and sucks up three heavy lines without stopping to breathe. "Ahh," she sighs, sniffling and straightening up, and smiling at me with her eyes just glazed.

"Are you Claire?" I say.

"No, Roberta," she says. "David's mistress."

"Oh."

"Hey," she says, and grabs my hand. "I got an idea. You want to go skinny-dipping?"

"I just went," I say.

"Good, you're in practice. You go ahead, I'll meet you at the pool. Be there in a few."

She turns back to the washstand, laying out more lines, and I wander on down the hall. Eventually I step through a swinging door into a bright tiled kitchen. The air is clouded with ganja smoke. A girl in shorts, T-shirt and almost-crewcut blonde hair turns from the stove, where she's cooking, and looks at me with a question in eyes that are laughing. She's standing up on one toe and twisting to look backward—I can see all her pretty curves and sways and arches. She reaches for a smoking reefer in an ashtray and takes a long draw on it, squinting at me through the smoke. Then she finishes and says, holding her breath, "Want some weed?" She holds it out. I shake my head and she says, "I'm

127

Claire. Maja told me she was bringing home a spicy meatball tonight."

"Her words or yours?"

"Her words, my impression."

I nod slowly and, watching her sway as she sets aside the reefer and picks up her knife, say, "I'll try not to do anything to disconcert your fantasies." I smile, I like her haircut and her smile and her eyes. Plus other things.

She hurries past me to the swinging door and peeks out. Then she comes back with a wise smile and pauses by me, speaking just above a whisper. "I got a couple hits of ecstasy stashed," she says. "Want to do 'em?"

"Hey, Claire," calls a man's young voice.

She glances toward the door. Still smiling, she points me toward another door. "Through there," she says. "I'll meet you by the pool."

Everyone seems to want me to go to the pool so I go. Also, there might be additional reasons. I sit on the end of the diving board in the dark, shivering, looking through the big windows into the abandoned living room. The steam rises up faintly around me, but when I lie on the board and reach down and trail my fingers in the pool the water feels too cold.

Someone comes into the living room and wanders toward the windows. She's small, dark and female. Very female. You can sense it through the glass. She's the exact opposite of me. She makes me remember the great Cuban poetess Benita Morales, who often told me, *"Hay que hacer mejor la raza."* Meaning, of course, that though similarities merely clash, opposites collide, and the sparks generated by the collision are startling, lovely, even eternal. At least, so she claimed. I wasn't convinced at the time. She said it so plaintively. It worked out finally, I discovered she was a transvestite and went on with no regrets. Or, at least, without those regrets. I could lie and say I have none. But I don't believe in lies. I don't believe in regrets either so it's a real dilemma. Don't worry. I'll work it out.

Benita's argument concerning the ecstatic annihilism of opposites didn't sway me at the time. But now I'm convinced. I stare at the small dark girl. She stares back, moving nearer and nearer to the glass. I never knew what it meant to want a woman before. And now, from the way she stares I know, for once, that I can finally have exactly what I want. She's already mine. It's a fact. I don't have to choose or decide. It was already decided, long before. Somehow. Somewhere. Destiny I guess. Something. Then, through the glass, I see her eyes shift subtly, and I know that she's not looking at me, but rather at her own reflection.

A tall, handsome young man comes into the living room with two opened bottles of long-necked Mexican beer. He resembles his father. The girl turns, he offers her the bottle in his left hand. She shakes her head, barely, and he shrugs, barely, and they disappear together.

The damp pool-mist rises, chilling me more and more. I stand up with my legs stiff and wobbly from sitting cross-legged, and walk unsteadily to the door I came out. That is, I think it's the door I came out. Something doesn't mesh. I'm standing in a huge amber-lit bedroom beside a vast waterbed built in the shape of a cross. A slender blonde woman sits at the foot of the cross, barely rising and falling with the gently undulating wave-action of the bed. There's a family resemblance here too. She's softly smiling with her mouth closed. She looks scary and beautiful in the amber light. Or, maybe, scared.

"I was watching you," she says in a husky voice. "I knew

you'd come."

"Are you Maja's sister?"

She chuckles and brings a goblet of deep-red wine to her lips, and sips. "Her mother," she murmurs. "Would you care for some wine?"

A door opens to my right, letting in a stark white light. A shrunken, bent gray form stands silhouetted. "Lucy," she says in a harsh commanding voice, "who is that furry blond man in the bathroom?"

Maja's mother sighs and watches me as she sips her wine. "That's David, Ma," she says.

"And who, might I ask," with her fists on her hips and her elbows angled outward, "is David? His body is almost entirely covered with tiny blond hairs."

"He's my husband."

"I see." The old woman nods thoughtfully. Then she spies me and her face lights up. "You're here!" she cries.

"Yes," I say, nodding.

"Who's that, Ma?"

"Your father, you ninny. I told you he'd be back any day—I've been wanting to talk to you, there's something I wanted to ask you." She smiles at me, half-sidelong, thrusting her hip toward me and winking. She glances toward her daughter, leans toward me and whispers, "Did you get the bread?"

"Uh, I guess I forgot," I whisper back.

"Now I told you not to come back without it," she says in a stern whisper. "You'll just have to go back." Then she smiles again, angling her head to the side and watching me from the corners of her eyes. "You're so impetuous," she says, "you haven't changed a bit. Now hurry, we'll all be waiting."

I leave the way she came and run into the young man from the living room.

"Hi, I'm Carlo," he says. "Claire wants me to spread the word, dinner's ready. Anybody else back there?"

We rendezvous at a big round table near the kitchen. Everyone is here. Maja sits on my left, Carlo on my right. Just past him I can see the small dark girl from the window. Her long thick hair tumbles down and she watches her plate, except for shy glances when her dark liquid eyes graze over you, catching momentarily. David sits at the end with his big tumbler. His mistress is on his right, then his silent Chinese secretary. Claire and her mother are going back and forth through the swinging doors to the kitchen. Maja's hand rests high on my thigh. I feel a bony grip fall on my left shoulder.

I glance up and back. The wizened gray woman leans over and whispers harshly in my ear, "Where's that bread? And what is that woman's hand doing on your leg?"

"Hey!" Maja calls loudly, making the old woman jump back. We glance at Maja. She's staring at Claire, who's laughing while she says something to the secretary or mistress, or both. She pauses and glances over.

"I'd like to know," says Maja, "what exactly my diaphragm was doing in with the dirty laundry."

"Since when is it my responsibility to keep track of your sexual devices and accessories?" says Claire, spinning toward the kitchen and trying not to laugh.

"You bitch—don't walk away when I'm talking to you!" Maja jumps up and chases her into the kitchen.

"Girls," says their mother and sighs and follows them in through the swinging door.

"They're all so full of shit," mutters Carlo, beside me. The shrunken gray woman taps him on the shoulder.

"Was that your hand I saw on my husband's leg?" she says.

"Is that your car out front?" he says to me.

"Yeah."

He asks another question I can't make out over the yelling and screeching in the kitchen. I shake my head. "What kind is it?" he repeats.

"A one-off."

"You mean like a prototype?"

"No, just something a friend and I put together."

"Really."

"Built it out of scrap," I say.

"From scratch?" He can't hear me either.

"Scrap. Junkyards, recycling centers, yard sales. Runs on alcohol. You know, eco-debt and all."

He nods like he knows. I glance across the table, where the secretary sits weeping quietly, glancing now and again toward David's end of the table. His mistress is asleep in her chair with her head thrown back, snoring softly. David sits gazing into near space, sipping from his big tumbler. Maybe he's thinking of something. Maybe not.

"Would you mind taking me for a drive sometime?" says Carlo.

"No problem. How 'bout now?"

"What?" he shouts, to be heard over an outburst from the kitchen.

"Let's get out of here," I say, leaning over and talking straight into his ear. He glances at the kitchen door, laughs, motions to the dark girl beside him and we three get up and walk out the front door.

You can hear the yelling from out on the porch and, slightly diminishing, on across the lawn to the car. I drag the toolbox up and fold the sleeping bag over it and we all climb in.

"State-of-the-art," says Carlo, grinning. The girl sits in the middle. Her bare brown arm brushes against mine as I drive.

"Runs quiet," he says. We rumble softly through the dark shaded streets.

"Yeah."

"How come you built a car?"

"We wanted to go fast." He nods and doesn't say anything. "Anyplace you want to go?"

"Let's see what's happening in Westwood," he says.

He gives me directions. The streets gradually become more and more crowded. Stoplights multiply. So do pedestrians, neon and noise. Long lines wrap around blocks from theater entrances. Crowds move back and forth with the WALK light. The street is packed. We barely creep, waiting for lights to change green and then not moving until after they change red again.

"We got to get out of here," I say. I'm starting to sweat.

"This sucks," says Carlo. "Sorry, man."

"What's the quickest way out?"

"Let me think."

We're stopped in the front row at a crosswalk packed with ambling young people. A crowd of college guys in sweaters and sport jackets roams past with the flow. A tall redheaded kid stares in through the front window of the car, ogling the girl. He shouts something I don't understand, making his friends laugh. They pause and stare in through the window with him. Carlo leans out the passenger window and shouts, "What'd you say?"

Someone from the crowd shouts something unintelligible and they all laugh. "Aw, screw you," mutters Carlo, sitting back in the car and waving them off.

"Hey fuck yourself, kid," yells the redhead, and kicks in

our right headlight.

"Fucker!" murmurs Carlo, opening his door. We both jump out at the same time and hurry forward alongside each side of the car—the crowd of guys bunches together and everyone else scatters. The light is changing and two cars honk. The redhead pulls a pistol from under his sweater and fires twice, aiming straight at Carlo's chest. Carlo goes down with the first shot and the second bullet wings a motorcyclist speeding up between the lanes behind him. The rider spins off backwards and the bike slams into the car beside us.

"Shit!" yells someone, I don't know who. Somebody screams. Everyone's running away, scattering at sharp angles. The redhead drops the pistol on the street and runs. I hurry around to the other side of the car and stare at the pavement. Carlo's gone. A bright white light shines in my face and I glance up. The motorcycle is coming straight at me. I jump back and he races by, lying forward over the tank with the engine winding out. It's Carlo.

I jump in the car and flip open the headers and stomp on the gas, peeling out after him. He slices between the lanes of traffic and I take heroic measures to keep him in sight, first swerving up onto an empty stretch of sidewalk for a quarter block, then pulling out into the oncoming lanes for eighty or ninety yards when nobody happens to be coming. We only run two lights and then we're threading through dark winding streets, running up close behind him with the engine roaring on the straights, falling back slightly on the curves. He rides and corners with the grace of a natural, like one born to speed.

The girl is in the back, thrown this way and that, scrambling to get hold of something solid before the next hard turn, and just missing. Now and then she mutters something

134

incomprehensible, in a foreign language. It resembles Spanish but I'm not sure. I'm not listening too closely, you've only got so much attention. I think she's crying, then she manages to climb back to the front, bracing herself against the dash and the edge of my seatback, and I glance over momentarily and see she's laughing.

He leads us up, twisting around and back and still up. We break out onto the spine of the ridge and fly twisting and winding above endless sparkling plains of distant glinting and shimmering lights. Finally he swerves to the right and parks on a narrow strip of dusty shoulder. We pull over after him and brake to a stop. I get out. He's bent over the bike, tearing off a chunk of chiggered fiberglass faring.

"You OK?" I say.

He pulls off the wrecked cowling and flings it over the bank, and turns to me with his eyes shining and streaming tears. "Wow!" he says, laughing.

"Where'd he hit you?"

"I ducked, man. I dodged a bullet. You got any credit cards?"

"No."

"I got to get to Texas. I know this girl in Corpus Christi. Oh well, I'll make it. That car's got some juice, how'd you keep up with me?"

"Wasn't easy. Where'd you learn to ride?"

"Me? I never been on a bike before." He laughs again. "I got to go," he says, and straddles the bike. "I'll see you." He fires it up and gooses the motor up to a whining purr.

"You got a gift," I say, but he doesn't hear me. "Hey—what about her?"

"Huh?" He glances back at the car. "Oh yeah." He grins and waves. "Sorry I can't introduce you, don't know her name. Seems like a nice girl though. 'Bye." He pulls onto the winding highway, lying down on the tank and opening the throttle, and fades away into the blur of distant lights and humming motors.

I walk back to the car and peel off a layer. We're blue now. In the night-light, a glossy shimmering blue-black. I get in. The girl sits on the padded toolbox, leaning back against the passenger door, watching me. She asks me, in Spanish, if I speak Spanish. I say yes (though I can't read or write it). She leans toward me, touches my arm lightly with her fingertips, and asks if I could take her to Hemet. Sure, why not. Oh good, she says, she's been trying for two days to get back to Hemet. I ask her where it is. She doesn't have any idea.

We wind down out of the dark hills back into the city and ask at a gas station. We ask at several. People aim us east and south. Finally someone names names, and numbers. We find a freeway and take it.

It's packed, as usual. Littered with blowing trash and drifting dust and detritus. We creep on and on. Finally we swerve around the ruins of a brass bedstead in the fast lane. After that the columns begin to thin out. Suddenly we're out of the city. We wind among dry hills. The freeway is abandoned. I open the headers and wind out the motor, topping 150, 160. The speedometer keeps climbing and in the curves we begin to float from one edge of the empty freeway to the other, using all four lanes. The windows are rolled down all the way and the hot wind blasts in and swirls around the car, lifting papers and pieces of everything and all useless clutter up and out, leaving us lighter and lighter. We float with the wide tires humming on a cushion of air and barely grazing the raised dots lining the lanes.

At last. Yes, this is the way it is. This is real. The warm dark countryside, a wide winding road, liquid air, and motion speeding forever faster, humming toward a limit that looks rushing upon you just like a wall, only at the moment of impact, hey, it's a window. We're through, and we're not even moving any more, we're at the center of the cyclone and it's everything around us that's spinning and swirling and whisked away into the impossible past, the imaginary future. We know where we are. Yes.

I look to the side, at the girl. She knows and looks at me. The car drives itself. No. There is no driving. We exist. Motion is only an idea. Necessity a neurosis. Desire a disease. I know now why I stopped believing in time. There's no believing in anything because, of course, it's impossible to believe in belief. Sorry. It's just not logical. It's never been simpler. We're free. It's wonderful. You can't believe what I'm saying, that I'm saying, or that there is such a thing as saying. It just doesn't matter. I smile. She laughs.

The freeway slims down to a highway and we lurch between distant stoplights, slowing to sixty for the crossings and then jacking it back up. Alfalfa blows in through the windows and finally we pull off into a field on a rutted track and hold each other tightly flesh-to-flesh. She holds me slightly tighter than I hold her. We lie naked on the glossy blue hood of the car with the creamy stars streaked across the sky and crickets singing from near and far. Low on the horizon behind us is the last of the orange glow of the city, like the sky over a distant fire. The warm air strokes every crevice. I do too.

She's from a little town in the Sonoran Desert and I ask her, Why not forget about Hemet, let's blast on past Palm Springs and out into open empty land, we'll cross the border somewhere east of Yuma Arizona and keep heading south and east. Yes, she says, and clasps me to her, reminding me of how women remind me of horses, the way they breathe and the measured hungry thrust and canter of their rumps and loins. Men only look like horses, and then only in dreams—they don't act like them. But women, with their alert fearful eyes, somehow blind, showing how part of their minds has gone on hiatus—they often seem magnificent, but a little stupid. Men don't have to pretend to stop thinking in order to mate. It's what they want and nobody ever pretended otherwise. Even when men go crazy, it's logical. We're consistent. The contract begins and ends all in the same elongated moment.

Women have it rougher. It's never really an ideal time. Nobody's guaranteeing that the flake will stick around more than a few minutes after the show's over. If a woman doesn't know how to drop off that analytical part of her mind she'll rarely have sex, rarely reproduce, and the trait dies out of the species. Sorry. But I'm not, really. Don't blame me, most of the time I'm trying to do my best, too. All right, so that's pretty damn lame. At least I'm not setting any glowing precedents that I'll have to try to live up to someday in the future. Which won't get here anyway.

She remembers suddenly: she has to stop in Hemet after all, to make sure her cousin is all right. He was wounded in a shootout with the police in Nogales. Which Nogales, I ask her. Mexican, she says.

We drive toward the dark warm horizon in front of us. Then from somewhere far behind or far in the back of my skull comes a tiny voice. "Get back here," says the small firm voice, gradually swelling louder and louder, and something in me snaps back, from the dark peaceful throbbing eastern horizon to the smoking orange skyline in the west.

"Well, yeah. Sure. I drove a couple thousand miles to get here."

"And, along the way somewhere, lost about ninety percent of your resolve."

"No, not at all. Not nearly that much. And, really, it was only after I got here that everything started changing on me. I think."

She sighs again, shaking her head. "Well, whenever. Take a look in the back."

I glance back. "Hey!" I yell, amazed. There are four skiis laid out among the six sculptures. "Where'd these come from?" I reach back and bring one forward. They're around 160 centimeters. I examine the ski, the pale marble-white top, the black base, the fine polished one-piece steel edge. I check the camber and stiffness, and lightness. I look at her. "This is incredible."

She shrugs. There's something almost like a smile about the cast of her mouth. Her eyes glance over, alive, deep, crystal clear.

"I've never seen skiis like this—where'd you get them?"

"I told you," she says, "I used to be an artist."

"What," I say and pause, groping for a notion. "You *made* these?"

She sighs again, looking ahead bored as hell, like, Why even try to converse with a moron?

"Jesus," I say, examining the ski I'm holding. We swing left and I'm pushed against the door. It swings open and I totter, grasping the ski with one hand and flailing with the other, but catching nothing. Her right hand shoots out and grips the ski, we both hold on and I pull myself back in. Blood from my hand and from hers smears from the sharp edges over the pearl-white surface, leaving smudged handprints.

She yanks on the brake, jerking us to a stop in the school parking lot.

"Be careful," she says.

We are directed to Room 4. I see them as soon as I step into the classroom with the first sculpture. Of course I recognize them instantly. They don't know me. But then, how could they? This time I make seven trips, bringing the skiis on the seventh.

We sit silently and I watch them. I see what's going on behind their faces. They look at the sculptures—especially the skiis—and at the artist, and at me. The two boys seem to take turns looking at each, as if their glances are somehow secretly choreographed. Then they glance at each other. And with each sequence of glances, you can see, they're leapfrogging each other.

My heart grows and shrivels and aches and glows and throbs and I want to weep and cry out and run over to them, enfold them in my long strong arms. But, no, not now. Not yet. There's a job to do. A message to pass along. Truth to impart. A new species to spawn. Are we the last of the last men, or the first of the first? That's for us to say.

"I was your age," I say to the class, but to the twins in particular, "when skateboards were first invented. We lived in the sticks, at first we only heard about them. Then kids came back from Christmas vacations in California with skateboards. Eventually stores began to sell them. When I was ten, we drove past a housing development built on a steep hill with brand-new smooth blacktop streets. My brother said that two kids from his high school rode skateboards down the smooth streets at speeds of thirty miles an hour.

"Naturally we were terrified to even imagine it. Especially

I—I've always been a chicken. I'm just like anybody else. Who could imagine going that fast, on a skinny board with the vibration chattering up through your ankles? I had nightmares thinking about it.

"Remember, this was a different age. Nobody was into this glam-boarding like you see around here. There were no gloves, no kneepads, no elbowpads. Nobody imagined skate-boarding in empty swimming pools, going over jumps, doing turns. This was the sixties and early seventies and every year the speed limit on the freeway went up ten miles an hour. There had never been any such thing as a gas shortage. In Arizona you could go 80, in Montana there was no speed limit at all. We were into going fast. The American Way. For us, skateboards were our first cars. Little cars, with no bodies. The engines were gravity. You wanted a bigger engine, you went out and found a bigger and steeper hill."

The kids are staring at me, they understand. Some are wide-eyed, some look a little dazed. That's how the teacher looks, sitting straight-up in her varnished wheeled chair. The twins are beyond all that. They watch me from identical faces, assured, eager, knowing. Somehow knowing all that they have yet to learn. They're with me. I get a glimpse of the artist, in her metal wheelchair. She's the only one not watching me. She's watching the twins. Her face resembles theirs. A family, or racial, resemblance. She seems to be smiling.

"Our boards were built for speed and they were long. My super-longie was the fastest we ever heard of and when I built it, it was my height: five-foot-two. We started off on the hills of Seahurst and Des Moines—not Des Moines Iowa. We went at night so we could see the headlights of cars before they came around the corner and creamed us, and so that the cops

143

couldn't see us. We wore our Dads' old retired heavy wool overcoats that always smelled of mothballs. Some kids wore their older brothers' scarred motorcycle helmets. I never wore any helmet at all. I wasn't there to fall. It wasn't a possibility. I had a mission.

"At first we were scared. Naturally. We started off, rolled downhill with the speed building and the vibration rattling up into our shins and knees—the boards had hard-wheels then and there was no padding in the mounts. Some kids put pads of rubber inner tube material under the mount to cushion it, but we couldn't sacrifice the control. Anyway, we'd go faster and faster until we were afraid we wouldn't be able to jump off, because we couldn't run that fast. So at the last minute we'd jump, run for a dozen yards till we could slow down, then turn around and catch the board coming down behind us.

"We kept pushing it. Closer and closer to the limit. Those first five steps your legs were *flying*, straining to keep up with your body and save you from skidding down the street on your face. Then finally someone—Atticus, naturally—rode it out. He just never jumped off. We all jumped, ran, picked up our boards—and stood there amazed, gazing way off down the hill after him as he disappeared around the lower curves, flying through the white glow under one streetlight after another. We glanced at each other, shrugged, got on our boards and followed him down. None of us jumped. We kept building speed. Soon we were going as fast as we could run. Then, faster! We were flying. The vibration in my legs disappeared. I kept watching ahead, dreading to see Atticus sprawled on the blacktop or crumpled in the ditch. My eyes streamed tears from the wind. Fear evaporated, I was filled with the feeling of wind and speed and there was no room

144

left for anything else, for thoughts, ideas, terror or anguish over what might happen, what might be, what might have been. There was no such thing—there was only what is. My ears were ringing with wild musical noise. It was the others, my friends, laughing. I was laughing too. We came to the bottom where the road flattened out by the beach. Atticus stood waiting, watching us, holding his longboard with the tail end resting on the blacktop, smiling.

"I set a speed record on my super-longie of 37 miles an hour. Atticus tried to break it. He wore an old white motorcycle helmet that night. I was following in the pace car. I saw his board catch a shimmy—in a flash he was off. Two steps and he went down. He ducked his head and flipped twice, then rolled and slid a while. He was covered with scabs for months and the helmet had deep parallel gouges from the top clear around to the back.

"Here's the funny part. That was the first time Atticus ever wore a helmet. Some people said he was lucky, some said he was jinxed. It's up to you to decide which."

I stop talking. The kids look at each other, then at their teacher. She sits dumbfounded. I look at the twins, whose bright eyes stay fixed on me.

"We'll need two of you to help carry this stuff," says the artist.

"We'll help," say both twins at the same time.

We carry the sculptures in two trips. At first we're silent. On the second trip I tell the boys, "Wasn't long before we moved on from skateboards to skiing, because the speeds were tripled. We joined ski patrol when we saw how the jerks in blue jackets with yellow crosses sewn on the back got to cut straight to the front of the line. They gave you one meal a day and a place to sleep and a free lift ticket. But cutting the lift-lines was the crux of the deal. On a good day the wait could run thirty or forty minutes. We never waited. Life is too short to wait in lines. It's against our religion.

"If you got caught jumping or skiing fast they kicked you off but hey, they had to catch you first. We lived for air and we swiped snowshovels from the hill patrol and built hoary jumps on the back runs. We kept to the trees and the chopped-up back trails because nobody skied there and there was no danger of coming across some injured tourist and having to deal with that. Who has time to deal with that?

"On skiis, gravity sucks you down and the skiis on the snow is what keeps you from going so fast you get killed. You fly down slicing through the folds and wrinkles and soft mounds. The earth pulls you down, it's like fusion. You learn about nuclear physics, empirically.

"It's like juggling globs of plutonium. How many balls can you keep in the air at once? I set a speed record bringing a toboggan down through Alpine Bowl to a skier with a wrenched knee. No turns. The victim refused to get in. He got up and skied down on his good leg. He yelled each time the splint skipped off a mogul. Later that day Atticus aimed to duplicate the feat but crashed and was run over by the toboggan. It careened into the trees and was smashed in a ravine. Nobody saw it happen and there was a big deal over the swiped toboggan. Atticus took me through the woods and showed me the wreckage. He was fifteen then. He lied about his age to get on the patrol."

We reach the van and I stop. Nobody says anything for a while. "Tell us another story," says one while the other nods.

Without saying anything they sit on the sill of the van's open side door and look up at me, chins in their palms and elbows resting on their knees.

"Yeah? You don't have to get going or anything?" They look at each other with a secret smile like they're sharing some private joke. "Ok, listen. There was lots of speculation over whether it was humanly possible to shoot Bonanza. The run comes down right under the chair. We believed they should use Bonanza for the downhill racing course. You want to see who can get down the mountain fastest or don't you? Everyone said that was stupid, a downhill isn't a drag race and besides, there is a fine line between downhill racing and suicide. Screw that. Why not tell the truth? You want to race or do you want to pretend to race?

"The mogulfield on the steepest part of the face sometimes got to look like the Himalayas. We never had a chance to try shooting it because the whole run was covered with sprawling geeks all day every day. Then finally they assigned us to Bonanza for the hillsweep.

"Usually they gave us some crusted-over back run in the sticks that nobody else wanted because they dreaded getting back to the lodge half an hour after everyone else. The hill captain usually hoarded Bonanza because it was the most direct line and he could be first back to the lodge. But one day his partner was a visitor from the Lake Tahoe patrol with blonde hair clear down to here and she—well, she had some attributes, that means good points—"

"Yeah, we know what that means."

"Yeah? Anyway, he swapped runs with us. We waited till everyone was gone. The chair-lift was stopped. It was snowing with a couple fresh inches on top of an ice base. We stood still and turned slowly white but inside my parka the sweat ran down my sides. Who'd be the first wimp to turn? Not I, Atticus.

"Finally he said 'What you waiting for?' and I said 'You.'

He took off. I skated hard trying to catch him and then dropped into my tuck as the hill fell away. He was just ahead on my left. We took the center of the short headwall on top and he kept his lead through the flats that emptied onto the face.

"I kept to the right hoping for a smoother border along the edge of the run. I was skimming the thick orange steel pylons that hold up the chair-lift. Atticus stuck to the middle of the run because he had a horror of dying plastered against the orange steel.

"We dropped down the face. He was skipping off the tops of the mountainous moguls like a rock skipping across choppy water. I plummeted down a narrow chute between the pylons and the trees. The orange poles ticked past on my left like telephone poles. My skiis bounced and clattered. They skipped and ricocheted and always ended up pointing straight down. Maybe I was airborne. I was goosey-loose and rigid at the same time. I was riding it out. The flats were rising up and stretching out in front of me, undulating with the slow breathing of the earth.

"It didn't work out for Atticus. They came up to get him with the Thiokol and took him down strapped to a board. One femur was poking through his thigh. The other leg only had a simple fracture. Four weeks later he cut the cast off the good leg with a hacksaw and I loaned him one of my old skiis. He only got in two runs. He quit at lunch because the body cast felt too much like a straightjacket. I helped him cut it off in time for the next weekend.

"The fastest anyone's ever gone on skiis is somewhere around 118. It's a good feeling. Nothing distracts you from what you're doing." I stop, not telling them the rest. Shooting Bonanza was all right. But even at the time I knew it was

148

possible to feel better. 118 just wasn't fast enough.

But that's not the kind of thing you tell someone. They'll have to find out for themselves. I make a third trip, bringing the four skiis. When I get back the boys are standing by the van, talking in shy quiet voices with the artist.

"These are for you," I say, handing two skiis to each of them. They take them, and holding one in each hand with the tails resting on the ground, they look them up and down with shining eyes.

"They're so light," says one.

"There's blood on mine," says the other.

"That's how we sign our work," says the artist. "See, they're handprints."

"How come only one has it?" says the first.

"You only sign one," she says. "The first of the series."

"You can trade off," I say. "Watch out for the edges, they're sharp. Do you live nearby?"

One nods, one points across the grass playground.

"These are valuable," I say. "Take them home now."

They nod again, watching me, wide-eyed.

"But they're only valuable if you use them," she says. "Promise me you'll use them, for skiing."

"We promise," they say.

I look at my boys and smile and fight not to let them see me cry. I want to hold them and know I can't. Then I get it, for once: of course, let them see. I shake hands with both, and I'm still smiling with the tears running down my cheeks. They watch me with their huge deep eyes. Then they run off across the mown playfield, cradling the skiis in their arms before them.

Finally it all makes sense. L.A., the capital of the world, the center of the center, the root of myth, a city at the end of the world, a smoking phoenix that the first man and his progeny might rise from the ashes of. To start a new race in a newer world.

Of course I'd find them here, in the thick of it. A ten thousand square-mile concentration camp, where the seeds are sown and someday, eventually, burst into flower. New beliefs. New ways. The purity of pure motion, total passion and intense extreme experience, the dream of the dream which, finally, becomes the most real of all imaginable and unimaginable realities. All coming to pass here, in L.A., in the festering humus mold, incubating the spores of the new race of man and spewing him (or her) out into the greater world from out of its seething oozing convulsion. We've started it now. It's inevitable. Two small boys, twins, running home across the fresh-mown lawn, breathless with their gift of magic skiis cradled in their arms and a tale of speed on their lips. They're of us now, among us, with us. They're us and ours. I sit in the van and we roll onto the freeway, smiling, knowing that all I ever dreamed of, is, and that worlds beyond my dreams are already coming to pass.

There's such a symmetry to it, to succeed just as I'm about to give up all hope, like the millions who entered the city before me. But I remember, thinking backward, that I felt on the brink of giving up many times, and instead always turned back from the edge and forged on. Often only barely, by the slightest nudge forward—but still, always forward. And I know that no matter how long or hard or impossible the struggle, the dream will inevitably win.

Then, rolling down the freeway in packed traffic at 35 to 45, as if like a sign, in the midst of the vast sprawling concentration camp of malls and business parks and housing developments, the land opens and the freeway leads us through a vast clearing with the green earth stretching out on either side, tilled and irrigated. I know now that victory is both sweet and inescapable, that the progeny will thrive and survive and lead a new people forward, and furthermore that before too many more smoky nights have passed in L.A., I will find my two and a quarter miles, and I will grace the smooth banked freeway with speeds in excess of mach point-25.

"Look at this," I say, marvelling. "Open land. Green. Farms. I can't believe it."

"I can," she says, and the deadness in her voice makes me glance over and I see, mirrored in her mask, the same death. "Seal Beach Naval Weapons Station," she says.

"What!" And I look closer and see the raised bunkers, spaced among the crops. "What the—this is only a few miles from the school!"

"Right."

"This is bullshit, there are thousands of people living all around this place. My sons—the school's downwind! Look at this, oh God, it stretches on for miles."

"Now you know," she says, "why the land is empty."

"If I took my sons and spirited them out of here, they'd say I was crazy."

"Paranoid," she says.

"If two weeks later a bunker blew and 30,000 people were vaporized, then who's crazy? Huh? Then who's paranoid?"

"They'd still say you were crazy," she says.

Red lights flash. "Damn, what the hell is this?" I say staring ahead.

The freeway is stopped. We brake hard, screeching and swerving a little and managing not to slam into anyone. Then we sit. Nothing moves. Even the motorcycles stop coming up the suicide lanes between the cars.

Nobody moves for hours. Then they start bleeding the cars off, one lane at a time. Cops are everywhere, their motorcycles leaning hard-over on their sidestands and their helmet chin straps hanging unclasped and the sweat soaking through their khaki shirts. Gas masks are slung loosely around their necks, ready to put on, with the small green air reservoirs strapped to their backs like little knapsacks. They're shouting, hoarse by now, Please keep moving, No cause for alarm, It's only fertilizer gas leaking from a farmer's shed. Nothing to worry about, just standard precautionary measures... They're organized, they have cones set up that angle us to the right and as we climb single-file up the off-ramp toward the overpass we see, far off among the bunkers, a crowd of hooded, white-robed milling figures, coping with the gas.

Nice of the navy to let the farmers use the land. But, hey, let's get it together guys. I mean, darn those farmers and their fertilizer gas! Oh well, just a minor inconvenience. Damned considerate of the government men to figure out right away what it's all about, and put our worries to rest. Maybe the fellows from the U.S. Information Agency have something to do with it. Good job. We all need more information.

We're shunted onto a surface street bordering the edge of the bunkerfield. Across the street on the right stands a high concrete wall surrounding a compound of condos and palm trees. A big sign says "Leisure World, Retirement Community." A whole world of leisure, right there inside the compound. How relaxing. Soothing, even. And on top of the twelve-foot wall, to make sure you're safe, they've even got barbed wire. The view across the street, through the barbed wire, is of wide open spaces: the Seal Beach Naval Weapons

Station. Great, where do I sign up? Do it now while you're still in your twenties. There's bound to be a long waiting list.

"I got to get out of here," I say with barely enough energy to murmur.

"What?"

And then I think, with waves of rage and outrage washing over me, Bullshit!

"Screw this," I say. "These cadavers, safe behind their barbed wire faces. All they want is their peace and quiet, their well-earned rest. They've spent millions of lifetimes perfecting the technique for sleeping through life. It's over before they ever knew it happened. And the thing about the Walking Dead is, until someone wakes you up—really jolts you the fuck awake—they like being dead. At least they think they like it. Well screw that. We're not going to let 'em. Sweet dreams? Hell no.

"I keep letting 'em almost run me out of here—but I got unfinished business to take care of. They keep trying to make me feel like I'm living in someone else's country. All the signs in foreign languages—and the signs in English are the most incomprehensible of all. Maybe that's why I stopped believing in signs, because they stopped making any sense. Screw 'em. I'm going to have it my way. I'm not leaving—not till I'm done here. I'm going to make it in the bigtime, right here on their turf—but on my terms. I won't let up I won't let it slide I refuse the hand that's dealt me I reject the terms! I name my own. I name true terms. I mean, what else is America here for? This is what it's all about, and keeps sliding away from. To hell with that. Go ahead, dream, aspire! That's what it used to mean, America. Or might have meant. What I believed it to mean, anyway. What I refuse to stop believing. Sorry, but—no I'm not. I happen to be right. That's all that matters. I don't care what anybody says or thinks or does. I know the way it's going to have to be. It's not even a matter of choice any more. There's the good guys and the bad guys. And me, I'm going to be an American."

I stop to breathe, shaking with rage and flushed with a strange interior heat, like lust.

"I came here to wake 'em up—and I'm going to. Everything they've done has been to try to put us all to sleep. And hey, it almost worked. I mean, look around. How many times have I caught myself just starting to nod off? Damned hard to wake up from a dreamless sleep. If nothing else works they'll finally resort to gas. Sleep, fucker! It's war. They almost won. Only they didn't. Come on, bring on the horseheads, the gentles, the swines. I'm ready for 'em. It's already over. It's been decided—*I* decided it. They're waking up. Tonight, tomorrow night, the night after—who knows when. Who cares! It's happening because I'm making it happen. It's not like I even have a choice. I'm an American, that's all."

"You're damned right," she says.

She rides with me tonight. We lash her wheelchair into place beside my seat, then lift her into it.

"Hey, you're getting fat," I say.

There's something about her face. I look quickly but miss it.

"Maybe I should go on a diet," she murmurs.

We're ready. We cruise the freeways, looking for that opening. We cross another freeway on an overpass, at right angles. A twelve-laner, six each way. A motorcycle cop has pulled someone over on the right shoulder just past the overpass. He's bent over his bike writing the ticket and the woman is out of her car, pacing. She drives a shiny red Japanese commuter model and she's wearing a business suit with a waistcoat and a tight little collar. She paces onto the bridge and as we drive past she vaults over the railing and off. She drops away toward the freeway below. She's gone. The cop never sees, writing away on the ticket. We're past. There's no going back on the freeway. Going to be a tie-up on the six-oh-whatever. Maybe you'll hear about it on the traffic report. I wonder if they'll mention the cause. "Woman's body jack-knifed in the slow lane."

They need us worse than I realized. It's already later than I thought. We drive on and on, between 35 and 50. The glimpse of daylight has to be up here somewhere. We're not finding it. We keep on. I feel a growing constriction in my chest. No, not a shrinking. A kind of swelling, cutting off my breath.

"Jesus," I say, "not this again."

"What?"

"I saw a baby die once. Did I tell you about it? I've never been the same. Never felt the same. It's like, suddenly I got asthma. And it always makes me think of that."

"Maybe you weren't the same before, either."

"What?" Breathing gets harder still, coming in wheezes that rasp my throat and upper lungs.

"Maybe everything makes sense, like you always thought it did—only for different reasons."

"I—what do you—oh, Jesus!" I gasp, with no air getting through at all and my vision blackening. I yank the wheel to the right, aiming for the shoulder. She's leaning over and gripping the wheel too, steadying it, aiming it. My foot stabs and gropes at the brake. We roll, slowing, coasting down toward a stop.

The throbbing ache in my chest blocks out everything else. I gasp and cough and try to say something, I have no idea what. Nothing important. Airrr, I need air. I suck at it and don't get any.

Then I see her clear porcelain mask, lowering toward me. It comes nearer and nearer, blurring in my eyes, looming massive and large and blacking out the world. Her face is everything. The dark Universe, the sun, blackness and death. It might be the last thing I ever see with these eyes.

Her mouth is on mine. I feel her soft lips seal against mine. I can even feel the tiny creases in hers lining up with mine, bonding, sealing tight—and then her tongue, wet and warm, encircling our mouths. I float, feeling nothing but that. Her, the opening to the world, my last lifeline thread. Then, gradually, easing from my chest I feel a loosening, a relaxation, a tingling hollowness that shimmers outward into the distant stretches of my toes and fingertips. Not a vacantness, but a fine, relaxed, easy emptiness. A release, as though certain things don't matter much any more. Don't matter at all. What things, I have no idea. That doesn't matter either.

Her mouth comes loose from mine, she pulls away. I breathe easy. Her face comes into focus before me, lit with pale freeway light. She's smiling.

"Jesus," I murmur and she laughs, a tinkling musical child's laugh, bubbling up out of her. "You're so beautiful," I say.

"Yes, you too," she says.

"I'm leaving. I guess it's over. Will you come with me?"

"No," she says, still smiling. "Now, I've got my own business to take care of."

"What business, where?"

"At the center."

"What center?"

"Of the center."

I help get her wheelchair out of the car and lift her into it. She touches my cheek, glancing up, with the headlights of the passing stream shining over us both. She smiles again, and turns and starts down the shoulder of the freeway, against the flow. Heading back in, toward the center.

I also have some business to take care of. I walk with that light floating feeling. I'm nimble, I'm quick. My peripheral vision is back, I can see over 180 degrees without twitching my eyeballs. I pull off the blue covering, leaving the car sheathed in rich glossy red. And I change the plates to my final set: original Alaska plates, with the Big Dipper pointing to the bright North Star. I pull in with the oozing rivertide. I stream with them, alert, awake. I'm ready.

I flow with the meandering freeway current. Gradually the cars ahead and around and behind me slow to a stop. We inch forward, then nobody moves. We inch forward some more, taking up the last of the slack. We're packed tight, so tight the motorcycles can't fit through the spaces between the lanes. There are no spaces, only solid metal suspended on rubber and air over the oil-stained gray-white concrete.

Nothing and nobody moves. Maybe this time they'll have to shut the freeway down for good. Abandoned to the rusting hulks and the rats and coyotes and pigeons and ravens and rattlesnakes and black-widow spiders that will come and make their dens and nests and tunnels through the rotting tires and parched and broken vinyl. A modern ruin, a monument to an idea that didn't work out.

I close my eyes when people start leaving their cars and walking away. They have to climb out through their windows because the doors are jammed handle-to-handle. From behind comes the shattering of glass as a man in a Delorean a few rows back kicks his way out through the windshield.

They filter toward the exits, climbing over the hoods and rooftops of the fossilized cars. The hollow clumping of their footsteps dies away and I wait, resting my eyes. Waiting for what? Good thing I don't believe in time. Lifetimes may be passing. Whole generations of microbes or insects in the Kalahari have surely lived and spawned and died while I wait.

It's dark when the grinding sound starts, from far back. I stir and look behind. A row of glittering white spotlights stabs across the sea of cars. They grow bigger and brighter, jolting and lurching. The noise grows too. The lights are mounted on D-9 Cats. A line of them comes grinding down the freeway, staggered like snowplows, clearing the freeway with their ten-foot angled blades, one lane per Cat. The lead bulldozer in the far-right lane clears a swath twelve feet wide, tossing and shoving the cars and trucks onto the next lane to the left—my lane. Behind him come the others, pushing the twisted heap farther and farther toward the left. The last Cat shoves the wreckage over the edge and down the shoulder.

They churn nearer. The stench of thick diesel exhaust wafts through the car. Their spotlights glare in through the rear window. I could get out and run for it, scrambling across the cars—no I can't. I slide low in my seat and grip the wheel and keep my eyes wide open as the lead Cat rumbles up alongside on my right. The car beside me is lifted, it slams into me and then crashes onto my roof—the ceiling sags and the right rear window disintegrates into a blur of tiny round glass crumbs and tinkles away. But the roof holds, it won't buckle. We built her strong, Atticus and I. The Cat's tank-treads clump by and there's open pavement on the right, carpeted with shattered glass and twisted bits of steel and chrome-painted plastic. I fire up the engine, crank the wheel

158

hard-over to the right and stomp on the gas. We lurch ahead and to the right and our sideways roll topples the car off our roof. I pull in behind the D-9 and follow him through, idling in first gear with no lights showing and the horses throbbing and rumbling and whinnying and just dying to get out and run.

The big Cat leads me to a junction where my frozen freeway butts into a still-oozing six-laner. I slip around the machine, hit the lights and slide into the flow. I creep along with them. None suspect what I've just escaped from. We stop and start. I measure our progress in glacial terms, in forward jolts of mere inches. Then we accelerate to a steady crawl, riding the clutch.

The sky ahead glows with a neon lustre. I inch slowly through wreckage strewn across the lanes. Hot-pink flares burn in bright straight dotted lines laid across the corrugated pavement in orderly, meaningless rows. We weave past fenders and bumpers and scattered pebbled glass and the burning and smoldering hulks of cars. A tanker-truck is jackknifed off to the right and hot orange flames shoot a thousand feet into the black sky. Red lights and blue lights and yellow lights flash and flare and spark in the darkness. Sirens scream and cops and medics run and yell and hooded firemen charge into the inferno shooting clouds of foam and billows of spray. The traffic cops stand by their motorcycles where they're parked along the lanelines, facing the oncoming traffic and motioning us past with rhythmic motions of a flashlight in each fist. I pass through, the light and noise fades. My single left headlight glares on the chrome bumper of the old white Mercedes ahead.

When I spot my opening, I seize it. The open lane stretches on into the black-shadowed distance. I swerve left, step on the gas and glance down to reach for the open-headers switch.

When I look back to the road a nondescript sedan is angling over ahead of me, swerving into my lane with no blinker flashing. It's too late to swing past—I curse and stomp at the brake. But there's no need—the intruder pulls away at speed, putting a couple dozen yards of bare concrete between us. My foot goes to the throttle and I press down, tentatively. The other keeps pulling away. I press harder. Now I'm jamming it to the floor. I'm holding steady, maybe gaining a fraction. Maybe not.

I follow the other down the concrete river, inching barely closer on the bends. The lights we pass fade to a blur. They disappear altogether. We're alone on the black-night freeway, using all three lanes, swinging from shoulder to shoulder and flying on through the headlighted darkness. I never glance to the speedometer. It just doesn't matter. We're flying.

And it doesn't matter, finally, that nobody's around to see it, to be dazed and dazzled, to be left restless and, perhaps, impregnated by the seething seed lodged in the base of their brain, beginning to sprout. It doesn't matter if anybody else ever knows or learns, really. Because I know. I have, finally, the experience of the experience.

I get past the other car on a long curving right-hander. That doesn't matter either. The other passes me. We go on and on. Then my fuel is exhausted and I roll to a stop on the left shoulder. I get out. I'm somewhere in a vast starlit desert land. Light enough to see, but not light enough to know what you're seeing. The other car comes back, driving the wrong way down the freeway, makes a swinging U-turn and comes up alongside. In the headlight illumination I see that the red covering has been peeled off my car from the wind. Underneath lies the glossy varnished inlay. Along the side is the coiled rattlesnake of the original American flag, and under that the inscription, "Don't Tread On Me, Either."

The other car stops. "Out of fuel," I say.

The other gets out and says, "No problem, I got plenty."

"I'm burning pure alcohol."

"Naturally. What else?"

We siphon some into my tank and speed off, leapfrogging each other through the night. The warm desert wind blasts through and the smooth banked concrete goes on and on, undulating across the earth. We're flying, way past 200 but that doesn't matter either. Numbers become meaningless, I don't believe in them any more. When the other runs out of fuel and coasts to a stop we siphon from my tank. When I run out again we siphon the other way. We drive on and on. I have no idea which direction. It doesn't matter. It never will.

THE BLACK ICE BOOKS SERIES

The Black Ice Books Series introduces readers to the new generation of dissident writers in revolt. Breaking out of the age-old traditions of mainstream literature, the voices published here are at once ribald, caustic, controversial, and inspirational. These books signal a reflowering of the art underground. They explore iconoclastic styles that celebrate life vis-a-vis the spirit of their unrelenting energy and anger. Similar to the recent explosion in the alternative music scene, these books point toward a new counter-culture rage that's just now finding its way into the mainstream discourse.

The Kafka Chronicles
A novel by Mark Amerika
The Kafka Chronicles investigates the world of passionate sexual experience while simultaneously ridiculing everything that is false and primitive in our contemporary political discourse. Mark Amerika's first novel ignites hyper-language that explores the relationship between style and substance, self and sexuality, and identity and difference. His energetic prose uses all available tracks, mixes vocabularies, and samples genres. Taking its cue from the recent explosion of angst-driven rage found in the alternative rock music scene, this book reveals the unsettled voice of America's next generation.

Mark Amerika's fiction has appeared in many magazines, including *Fiction International, Witness,* the German publication *Lettre International*, and *Black Ice*, of which he is editor. He is presently writing a "violent concerto for deconstructive guitar" in Boulder, Colorado.

"Mark Amerika not only plays music—the rhythm, the sound of his words and sentences—he plays verbal meanings as if they're music. I'm not just talking about music. Amerika is showing us that William Burroughs came out of jazz knowledge and that now everything's political—and everything's coming out through the lens of sexuality..."

—*Kathy Acker*

Paper, ISBN: 0-932511-54-6, $7.00

Revelation Countdown

Short Fiction by Cris Mazza

While in many ways reaffirming the mythic dimension of being on the road already romanticized in American pop and folk culture, *Revelation Countdown* also subtly undermines that view. These stories project onto the open road not the nirvana of personal freedom, but rather a type of freedom more closely resembling loss of control. Being in constant motion and passing through new environments destabilizes life, casts it out of phase, heightens perception, skews reactions. Every little problem is magnified to overwhelming dimensions; events segue from slow motion to fast forward; background noises intrude, causing perpetual wee-hour insomnia. In such an atmosphere, the title *Revelation Countdown*, borrowed from a roadside sign in Tennessee, proves prophetic: It may not arrive at 7:30, but revelation will inevitably find the traveler.

Cris Mazza is the author of two previous collections of short fiction, *Animal Acts* and *Is It Sexual Harassment Yet?* and a novel, *How to Leave a Country*. She has resided in Brooklyn, New York; Clarksville, Tennessee; and Meadville, Pennsylvania; but she has always lived in San Diego, California.

"...fictions that are remarkable for the force and freedom of their imaginative style."

—New York Times Book Review

Paper, ISBN: 0-932511-73-2, $7.00

Damned Right

A novel by Bayard Johnson

Damned Right is a visceral new incarnation of the American road novel. Its twentysomething protagonist practices the religion of speed and motion, judging his every action by one question: Is it right? The freeways beyond his home in the Pacific Northwest call to him with their promise of a wide-open throttle and infidels to outrun. In a mountain community hard against the Canadian border, he attempts to save the life of a dying infant. This child forces a question into his heart, and, without fully understanding his mission, he is compelled to head south to discover the answer. The bleak sprawl of Los Angeles, a city of idealists imprisoned by their own fossilized dreams, lies ahead of him, drawing him into a series of adventures and ordeals and revealing to him an apocolyptic vision of the future.

Bayard Johnson has written more than sixty short stories, five movies, and over 220 songs. Three of his stage plays have been produced in small theaters in Los Angeles. Early in 1993, Johnson and AIM activist Russell Means formed Treaty Productions, with the intent of producing motion pictures promoting equality, brotherhood, and justice.

"When you hunker down with this book *Damned Right* you better buckle-up seat belt, don crash helmet....He's a reckless rider swerving words under the influence of semantic juices Kerouac never dreamed of!"

—*Dr. Timothy Leary*

Paper, ISBN : 0-932511-84-8, $7.00

Avant-Pop:
Fiction for a Daydream Nation
Edited by Larry McCaffery

In *Avant-Pop*, Larry McCaffery has assembled a collection of innovative fiction, comic book art, illustrations, and other unclassifiable texts written by the most radical, subversive, literary talents of the postmodern new wave. The authors included here vary in background, from those with well-established reputations as cult figures in the pop underground (Samuel R. Delany, Kathy Acker, Ferret, Derek Pell, Harold Jaffe), and important new figures who have gained prominence since the late eighties (Mark Leyner, Eurudice, William T. Vollmann), to, finally, the most promising new kids on the block. *Avant-Pop* is meant to send a collective wake-up call to all those readers who spent the last decade nodding off, along with the rest of America's daydream nation. To those readers and critics who have decried the absence of genuinely radicalized art capable of liberating people from the bland roles and assumptions they've accepted in our B-movie society of the spectacle, *Avant-Pop* announces that reports about the death of a literary avant-garde have been greatly exaggerated.

Larry McCaffery's most recent books include *Storming the*

Reality Studio: A Casebook of Cyberpunk and Postmodern SF and *Across the Wounded Galaxies: Interviews with Contemporary American SF Writers.*
Paper, ISBN: 0-932511-72-44, $7.00

New Noir
Stories by John Shirley
In *New Noir*, John Shirley, like a postmodern Edgar Allen Poe, depicts minds deformed into fantastic configurations by the pressure, the very weight, of an entire society bearing down on them. "Jody and Annie on TV," selected by the editor of *Mystery Scene* as "perhaps the most important story...in years in the crime fiction genre," reflects the fact that whole segments of zeitgeist and personal psychology have been supplanted by the mass media, that the average kid on the streets in Los Angeles is in a radical crisis of exploded self-image, and that life really is meaningless for millions. The stories here also bring to mind Elmore Leonard and the better crime novelists, but John Shirley—unlike writers who attempt to extrapolate from peripheral observation and research—bases his stories on his personal experience of extreme people and extreme mental states, and his struggle with the seductions of drugs, crime, prostitution, and violence.

John Shirley has been a lead singer in a rock bank, Obsession, writes lyrics for various bands, including Blue Oyster Cult, and in his spare time records with the Panther Moderns. He is the author of numerous works in a variety of genres; his story collection *Heatseeker* was chosen by the Locus Reader's Poll as one of the best collections of 1989. His latest novel is *Wetbones.*

"John Shirley serves up the bloody heart of a rotting society with the aplomb of an Aztec surgeon on Dexedrine."
—*ALA Booklist*
Paper, ISBN: 0-932511-55-4, $7.00

The Ethiopian Exhibition
A novel by D.N. Stuefloten
While World War II rages in Europe, John Twelve climbs onto a four-cylinder Indian motorcycle and crosses Ethiopia, searching for truth, for beauty, for mystery. At the same time, a modern American girl strolls the streets of Puerto Vallarta, where she is accosted by a film director—actually Ahmed, an Ethiopian murderer. He is making a film, he explains, about a man crossing the Ethiopian desert on a motorcycle. The girl accepts a starring role—and with this embarks on an adventure that takes her beyond the limits of ordinary reality. Her companions on this mystery tour include Sheba, the 3,000-year-old Queen of Ethiopia; Prester John, the legendary King of Ethiopia; and the Emperor Haile Selassie, the Conquering Lion of Judah. The innocent American girl, now called Dominique, watches in amazement and alarm as the world reveals an esoteric reality that she never knew existed.

D.N. Stuefloten has spent most of his life wandering around the world writing novels. He has been a magician's assistant in Africa, the manager of a mining company in Borneo, a fisherman in the south seas, and a smuggler in India. His first novel, *Maya,* was published in 1992 by Fiction Collective Two. Paper, ISBN: 0-932511-85-6, $7.00

Doggy Bag
Stories by Ronald Sukenick
Doggy Bag is a contemporary answer to T.S. Eliot's "The Waste Land"—don't waste anything. It forges an Avant-Pop credo from recycled scraps of American mass culture. In the age of the consumer, the American tourists in this series of interconnected stories are still trying to buy answers in Europe, but finally they're forced to conclude that whatever they're looking for isn't there. These travelers must turn back to what they know best, sampling the entertainment industry, B-movie versions of ancient mythologies, urban myth, advertising, and popular lore. They communicate their findings through cryptograms, secret codes, and strange graphic designs. Along the way they encounter Federico Fellini, Jim Morrison, a bird named Edgar

Allan Crow, a secret sect of White Voodoo Financial Wizards, humans infected with a computer virus, the Iron Sphincters, the Guardian Angel Mind Liberation Unit, the Wolfman, Total Control, Inc., and Bruno the sex dog, among other bizarre phenomena. The characters in these stories—from the New World in more senses than one—have no choice but to attempt to sort out a fresh spiritual commitment from the confused sound bites of a channel surfer's nightmare. They summon the reader to join a shadowy conspiracy in support of traditional American values of liberation and freedom.

Ronald Sukenick has previously published ten books, among them *Down and In, Up,* and *Blown Away.* He is the publisher of *American Book Review* and of *Black Ice* magazine, as well as codirector of Fiction Collective Two. He lives in Boulder, Colorado; New York; and Paris; and is a professor at the University of Colorado.

Paper, ISBN: 0-932511-82-1, $7.00

Individuals may order any or all of the Black Ice Book series directly from Fiction Collective Two, Publication Unit, Illinois State University, Campus Box 4241, Normal, IL 61790-4241. (Check or money order only, made payable to Fiction Collective Two.) Bookstore, library, and text orders must be placed through the distributor: The Talman Company, Inc., 131 Spring Street, #201 E-N, New York, NY 10012; Customer Service: 800/537-8894.